The
Good McCoy Lad

by

Toni V. Sweeney

The McCoys, Book 2

The Wild Rose Press, Inc.
PO Box 708
Adams Basin, NY 14410-0708
Visit us at www.thewildrosepress.com

Publishing History
First Edition, 2024
Trade Paperback ISBN 978-1-5092-5718-8
Digital ISBN 978-1-5092-5719-5

The McCoys, Book 2
Published in the United States of America

Chapter 1

Spring, 1860

"And this, my dear, is Mr. Quinton McCoy…and his sons…"

"McCoy?" The older lady in the party spoke.

Surely not Lord Alisdaire's wife, but perhaps his mother? Colin decided.

She was gowned as lavishly as the others but in more subdued tones, deep maroon, almost black, trimmed in ebony lace interspersed with jet beads. Her hair was snowy-white, and though she wasn't very wrinkled or waddled, her movements and voice bespoke much more age than His Lordship.

"Not related to that rapscallion Padraig McCoy, I hope?" she asked, in a tone carrying past their little group and seeming to echo about the hall. "The one Lord Cornwell might've challenged to a duel if he could've caught him?"

"I say…is that true, Quinton?" Robert William Cleary, Lord Alisdaire, asked, interest quickening at a bit of gossip.

In spite of his surname, he sounded very English.

"My second son," Quinton admitted, glancing around and seeing with relief no one else paid attention to her question.

"Not the same one I wrote to the Vice-Chancellor of

Oxford about? To keep the boy from being expelled?"

"The same, I'm sorry to say." Quinton's answer was a bare murmur.

Even absent, Padraig was a source of embarrassment to his father. Quinton couldn't very well deny the relationship. Everyone was aware of it, for the McCoys had lived in Tipperary long before Quinton's grandfather was born, and all his sons had grown up there.

"We don't speak of him." Donal, looking dour and formal, interjected in his well-modulated and very British-sounding tones, being careful not to allow any tinge of reprimand in his voice. After all, he was speaking to a nobleman.

Colin thought Donal looked perfect. He had to admire his brother's choice of garments. The only item of clothing breaking the black monochrome of his evening clothes were his white shirt and the embroidery on his satin waistcoat.

"You've a right to be afraid," the dowager Baroness Alisdaire retorted. "From all I've heard, that boy was full of dash-fire, but deserving of the infernal cut, not only by our entire society but also his family."

"Good God, Mother, where do you get those phrases?" Alisdaire asked. "You sound as if you've been hobnobbing with the footmen again."

"You should try it, Robert," the old lady rejoined. "That's the best way to get the gossip while it's still fresh."

"Where's the lad now?" Alisdaire inquired, calmly ignoring Donal's statement as well as Quinton's scowl at his pursuing the subject of his second son.

Briefly, Colin was glad his mother and sister-in-law

weren't with them but had been left chatting inside, with some other matrons in a little group gathered near the edge of the ballroom.

"Padraig is no longer here," Donal said quickly, his expression denoting plainly he hoped that would end the conversation.

"Lord, you don't mean he finally got his?" Alisdaire looked surprised but not sympathetic, rather greedy for more details. "Which one of the cuckolds did it?"

"Robert!" Lady Alisdaire spoke for the first time.

She was near the same age as her husband but still slim and handsome. Her gown, in contrast to her mother-in-law's, was of that delicious but poisonous arsenic green, tricked out with gold braid and peridots on the sleeves and down the bodice, as well as on the border of the hem. Behind her, waiting impatiently, stood the other member of their party, the girl Colin most especially wanted to meet.

"Eh?" Alisdaire looked at his wife as if he had no idea what she meant.

She inclined her head slightly and shook it. He looked away.

"Sorry…didn't mean to…"

"'Tis quite all right." Quinton's hasty answer implied it most certainly was not all right but he wasn't about to admit it and insult the gentleman by hinting he was thoughtless and unfeeling as well as something of a gossipmonger. "Padraig is still alive, but he's gone from Tipperary, from th' whole o' Ireland, in fact."

"The last we heard, he was somewhere in America," Donal explained, his precise tones contrasting so distinctly with his father's Irish slur.

Colin felt himself bristle a bit, as he always did when

his brother and father were speaking to others, because of the contrast in their speech.

It was a sore point between them. Donal said he merely spoke that way out of habit, because all his fellows at university and his current acquaintances did. Colin countered that once he graduated, he should've reverted to *normal* speech, namely an Irish accent, but such obviously hadn't been the case.

"A place in the central-western part of the country, called Nebraska."

"United States, eh?" Alisdaire looked even more interested. "Never been there. Like to go, though…on one of those buffalo hunts…"

"Father, could we please change the subject?" A much younger voice intruded, also British but soft and melodious.

Colin's heart speeded up a bit at the sound. He turned toward its source. The daughter, petite as her mother, but oh so young. The moment he saw her, his interest immediately perked. Seeing that, Donal reminded him she was being presented tonight. This was her first ball, and while the season in Tipperary might not be as grand and glorious as its London counterpart, it was equally important to all the young women making their debuts. Later, some of them would go on to England and be presented again, as no doubt this young lady would certainly do.

"Advertising her availability for marriage in two countries," Donal said.

Baiting her traps for the bachelor prey of two countries, Colin would've corrected. It gave him a bit of a twinge knowing he was now included in that group, and even more of one because as soon as the little group came through the door, being helped out of their capes and shawls by servants stationed for that specific purpose, he knew he had to meet the girl.

Donal's quiet explanation hadn't set his heart a-pittering, but the girl's looks had. She was exquisite. *All right, admit it, Col, ol' man, you're sniffin' around the trap an' not payin' attention to how sharp its teeth are.*

He decided he had to have a dance with her, perhaps several, before the other young men at the ball discovered her. This wasn't Colin's first ball in Tipperary, but young men entering the season as eligible bachelors weren't designated as such. They simply appeared, and went on their way through the obstacle course, relying on their older brothers, cousins, or friends to help them survive by offering advice and warnings as they were introduced, dancing their way among the array of eager, marriageable young women.

"You promised us no gossiping tonight," the girl continued.

She was dressed in a fashionable but typical debutante's ball gown, white as most of the other young women wore. Hers, however, was embellished with pink bruxelles lace and tiny ribbon rosettes nestled into the folds of her overskirt and sleeves, giving it enough color to make her stand out in the overwhelmingly blanched crowd around them.

"Now you're doing exactly that, and leaving us standing here unintroduced." She glanced around, caught Colin's eye, and dimpled.

Her gaze took in his appearance, starting at his elaborate white cravat and traveling down his stovepipe evening trousers, every bit as stylish and formal as his brother's but seemingly worn with much more flair and animation even while he was still. Colin felt he'd been weighed and definitely not found wanting but given a great amount of silent approval.

"Do I have to present myself to this gentleman?" She looked directly at him. Her eyes were blue, like the sky at noon, contrasting with her deep brown, almost sable hair, twisted into thick curls at the back of her head with little tendrils escaping to drape in front of her ears and at the nape of her neck.

Follow-me-lad curls, Donal would've called them.

A challenge? Definitely, as if she'd tossed one of those delicate white kid gauntlets at his feet.

"Don't you dare!" Her mother appeared scandalized. "That's forward."

"Since it appears that's the case, allow me to assist you."

Ignoring Lady Alisdaire's words while feeling everyone's gaze upon him, especially his father's, Colin accepted the challenge.

"Then we'll be known to each other." He inclined his head, feeling a curl slip forward and dangle over his right eye. He ignored both it and the irritation it engendered. "Colin McCoy. Esquire."

"How do you do, Mr. McCoy?" She smiled and the dimple grew deeper. She held out her hand and he grasped it gently, bowing over it as she dipped a curtsey. "I'm Fiona Cleary…the Honorable Fiona Cleary."

"Miss Fiona." He clasped her hand a little firmer, tight enough to feel the warmth of her fingers through the glove.

"That's enough of that." The dowager placed a hand over theirs, pushing them down and apart. "You've been bold enough, girl. What will people think?"

"That I'm doing what my father won't?"

Lord Alisdaire coughed, loudly and not discreetly. "As I was about to say before I was so rudely interrupted…" He ignored the fact that he'd interrupted himself with the tangent about Quinton's wayward son. "This is Donal…"

Donal performed a bow, exact enough to be gracious, but with enough restraint to prevent a flourish.

Good ol' Donal, Colin was envious. *Perfect. Always perfect.* He gave his attention to His Lordship, readying himself to be acknowledged and give his own bow.

"..and…uh…"

Not again. Colin struggled to keep his anger out of his expression.

"This is my third son, Colin," Quinton supplied.

"Colin, of course." Lord Alisdaire made a sound suspiciously like a hiccough which might be his version of a laugh. "You've so many, I sometimes forget their names." He looked at Colin. "My apologies, lad."

"Quite all right, sir." Colin tossed aside any attempts at bowing and merely nodded. So much for impressing anyone with his manners. *Da has only three sons*, he mentally corrected His Lordship. Two now, with Padraig exiled as he was.

His Lordship took a deep breath, preparatory to continuing what he'd been saying.

"Lord Alisdaire." Colin cut him off before he could utter the first syllable. "Now that our identities are established, would you allow me to escort Miss Fiona to the dance floor?" He cocked his head slightly, catching the beginning notes of something lively. "I believe the first dance is starting."

Her Ladyship looked as if she might object, but His

Lordship nodded.

"Of course, lad." He caught Fiona's hand, patted it, and placed it in Colin's.

Inside his glove, Colin's own fingers tingled. He wondered if that was a *Sign*. Gently, he settled Fiona's hand on his arm and escorted her through the door and into the ballroom, leaving his father and brother to brave whatever else was coming from His Lordship. He passed Donal's wife and his mother, coming out to join the others, and ignored them.

Behind him, he heard Her Ladyship remonstrating with her husband on the impropriety of what had happened, as well as Alisdaire's reply.

"Don't matter. They're introduced, and the girl's out there where everyone can see her. That's what we're here for, ain't it?"

Indeed.

****

Quinton Aloysius Francis Xavier McCoy was a member of Ireland's landed gentry. His people had come to the island with members of the Uí Néill clan who claimed the throne of Ulster. They'd been warriors and men to be reckoned with. They were also men who appreciated beautiful women and a good many became notorious as lovers…of both their own women and a good many other men's. It was a joke in the McCoy family that so many duels had been fought in the name of love it was a wonder any of the males survived to perpetuate the family name.

A good many did survive, however, and Quinton was currently head of the family in that section of the kingdom. It wasn't as it had been long ago. Now, though he was a landowner in his own right, he was, for all intents and purposes, also Lord Alisdaire's steward, his acting estate manager, taking care of business in his Lordship's absence.

Where some might've considered it a disgrace to take orders from a fellow Irishman more English than not—an educated Irishman at that—by collecting rents, maintaining the farms for His Lordship, and doing all the things he should have been doing for himself, Quinton recognized that if he refused to do it, it might fall to another from across the waters, and that one, not being Irish-born and bred, would be more harsh with the tenants hereabouts. Quinton was as proud as the next man, of both his name and his family, except for Padraig, of course, but he had the sense to know when to ignore his pride if it were best for everyone's welfare.

Lord Alisdaire had gained the land estate through various means. The major part came to him upon the death of the most recent lord, an absentee landlord who had resided in County Cork and had gone to his reward a few decades earlier. Since there were no heirs, the title died out also, but Alisdaire, being a far-distant relative, inherited the land and was instated as landlord. He proceeded to win more by buying up gambling markers, while other lands had been bought when the current owners died and the estates and surrounds were sold to pay debts. Other parcels had been presented to him by the English Crown because it was unclaimed by anyone.

Whatever the reason, Quinton reckoned it was best for all involved if he accepted the position Alisdaire offered him and made as little protest as possible. The farmers and tenants weren't exactly happy about coming under a new landlord's sway, but once Quinton made them see that as long as he was in charge and Alisdaire, who spent a scant three months in the county, remained more or less absent, things would go on as they always had.

At this time, Quinton was just approaching a vigorous middle-age, being a little more than two score and ten. He'd been a bit of a rogue in his youth, but that was barely spoken of now, and then only by some of the oldsters who remembered what laments his father had concerning his eldest son. Perhaps that was why Quinton had been so heavy-handed with Padraig, whom he saw as a reflection of his younger self. Nevertheless, he'd married long before he could be considered dissolute or a wastrel, and now had three sons and a daughter.

Donal, his eldest and heir, had been sent to school in England where he became more British than the most homegrown John Bull. Upon graduation, he stayed in London and seemed in no hurry to marry. It was only at Quinton's harping on having a grandchild with the McCoy name that Donal finally became betrothed to an English lass to whom he had now been wed for ten years.

Padraig, the second son, was the designated black sheep of the family, by birth order and temperament. He had been mischievous as a youngster and failed to grow out of it as a young man. Padraig chose to attend Oxford, protesting being sent to Cambridge mainly because Donal was matriculating there. Hearing his brother's affected speech after his first return home on holiday, Padraig stated quite vehemently he wanted nothing to do with a place of learning making Irishmen sound like Englishmen. Though Quinton reminded him Oxford might do the same thing, he resisted strenuously and retained his native accent, much to his elder brother's dismay whenever he had to introduce him to any of his friends…which he did as little as possible.

At school, Padraig had already gotten a reputation as a trickster and a cony-catcher as well as a youngster intent on following in the McCoy family tradition of a man who loved women. In Quinton's opinion, he was fast on his way to becoming a libertine, and he despaired of how the boy would turn out once he graduated and was released into the world.

To his father's chagrin, Padraig didn't graduate. After a near-expulsion, avoided only through his father's fast thinking and the aforementioned letter by Lord Alisdaire, he came home on holiday, discovered too many Englishmen in the vicinity who were practically begging to be relieved of their money by legal, if highly questionable means, and didn't return to school.

Quinton spent a good deal of his time paying off debts and soothing British sensibilities. It was also unfortunate that a good many of those men had neglected wives whom Padraig felt it his duty to soothe.

Finally, the miscreant went one step too far and diddled one wife too many.

Lord Cornwell was a good friend of Lord Alisdaire, and he could, with a single word, threaten Quinton's own position as steward. Quinton did the only thing he could to save himself and the people he considered under his protection. He banished Padraig, promising him a substantial cheque each month as long as he left Tipperary and never came back. Padraig agreed and became a remittance man, a disgrace paid to stay away from his family.

He had been gone almost a decade now and Tipperary had been extremely quiet in all that time.

Being closer in age to Padraig than to Donal, Colin

always looked up to his elder brother. It was a great blow to the youngster when Padraig left home at Quinton's insistence. Colin was only eighteen at the time, and had been eager to join his brother in adult adventures as soon as he was older. As it was, he was sent to Eton, to be alternately ignored and bullied by Donal, who despaired of having a young brother insisting on also clinging to his accent and becoming as little of a gentleman as possible.

Colin did both his brothers one better in the speech department, however. When in public, he affected as British an accent as Donal's. At home, he was as Irish as they came, a bit of a bother for the boy but a relatively happy medium for all involved.

That Colin became any kind of gentleman at all and had been allowed at the ball at which he met Fiona Cleary his older brother considered nothing short of a miracle.

Colin had expected to live in London as Donal was doing. However, after graduation and the expected Grand Tour—where, to his chagrin, his father insisted on accompanying him—Quinton informed him he was to stay in Tipperary. Otherwise, funds for his personal entertainments would be severely curtailed. No reason was given. Colin was suspiciously certain Quinton feared he was attempting to follow in his wayward brother's footsteps, though he as yet had no scandal attached to his name. Perhaps Quinton was simply making certain it stayed that way.

Whatever the reason, Colin was home to stay, at his father's iron-bound request.

That was the current situation, where the McCoy offspring were concerned. Donal was married and settled; Padraig was out of the picture altogether; Colin was at home and under his father's thumb, and his daughter...? Bridget Megan was a quiet girl, and obedient, doing what her father wished without dissent. She was married to a man he'd chosen, another landholder, strengthening Quinton's claim to this part of Ireland.

****

In the ballroom, a *contredanse* was in progress. Performing the intricate whirls and turns and weaving under other dancers' arms as they formed arches definitely kept one concentrating on the dance and held his attention. The only time Colin actually managed to speak to Fiona was when they came together and momentarily spun each other about.

During one of those times, Fiona said, "You dance very well, Mr. McCoy."

"Why do you sound surprised?" he asked, green eyes twinkling. He was puffing slightly. The dance was a lively one.

"Do I?" She frowned and that made the dimple reappear.

Colin was delighted.

"I certainly didn't mean to."

"Ah, I think you were expecting me to fall over my own feet...because I'm such a clumsy country oaf." He'd pondered which accent to use with her, then decided a slight blending of both might work better. "...either that or because I'm bedazzled to be dancing with such a beautiful lass."

"You're..."

The rest of what she'd been about to say went unspoken as she turned away following the steps of the dance. Colin performed the next section, somewhat rudely keeping his head turned and his eyes on Fiona instead of his current partner until they were together again.

"You're making light of what I said," she finished as if they'd never been parted.

"Indeed, I was," he agreed. "But that last was true. I *am* dancing with the most beautiful lass here."

"Thank you." She curtseyed as the last notes sounded and the dance ended.

Fiona started past him, only to stop as Colin caught her arm.

"Wait."

She looked up at him, then down at his hand. She appeared slightly startled by his detaining her. He released her before anyone could take note.

"Another dance will be starting. Stay and grace me with it also."

Briefly, their eyes met.

"Very well."

The strains of the violins floated across the dance floor.

"A waltz?" Fiona looked surprised.

"Surely your parents allow you to dance it?" Colin certainly hoped so. To be able to put his arms around that white satin waist… "'Tis been accepted for years now. Even Almack's allows it, and has for some time." Again, his eyes twinkled. "Or is it that you don't know how?"

"I know how to waltz." Her chin lifted. "And my parents don't mind if I dance it…with a *gentleman*." She stressed that word slightly. "Are you a gentleman, Mr. McCoy?"

"Certainly I am." He pretended a bit of a huff. "I'm

not my brother." *Padraig, forgive me,* he mentally prayed.

Taking her hand, he swung her into his arms, one hand sliding to her waist. His fingers played hesitantly against her ribs a moment before settling into a gentle clasp, just tight enough for Fiona to be aware of his touch. Colin listened briefly to the music, nodded, then swung Fiona into the first step.

"Do you like waltzing, Miss Cleary?" he asked after they completed one rotation.

"Yes, I do, Mr. McCoy." She was telling the truth if the gleam in her eyes was any indication. "It's so smooth, like ice skating."

"Ah, but when you stop, 'tisn't with the same sudden shock." He smiled. "And if you fall, there's no cold ice to freeze your…" He paused, then continued as she looked up at him quickly, "…your smile."

Momentarily, Fiona looked uncertain, then she laughed.

"I like waltzing, also," he continued. "Do you know why?"

"Because the music is so beautiful?" she guessed.

"Nay…because 'tis the only time I can hold a woman in my arms and feel her body moving against mine and not be accused of being lewd."

He didn't add that, in spite of his age, he'd only rarely had the pleasure of feeling a woman's body against his when not in a dance, and a couple of those times was thanks to Donal.

"You shouldn't say such things," she protested, looking away.

"Shouldn't I? Then my abject apologies. I stand corrected."

That made her look back at him, eyes searching his briefly.

Colin glanced around, trying to ascertain where Quinton and Lord Alisdaire were. He found them standing in a group, one speaking vociferously, almost on the point of argument, the other listening. Lady Alisdaire and the dowager were a short distance away, seated on a velvet settee. Several women, including Colin's mother and Donal's wife Felicity, hovered around them as they pontificated on some subject.

"Given encouragement, I believe you might be a scoundrel, Mr. McCoy," she accused.

"I?" He shook his head, and was struck by her expression, both timorous and eager, and thought how very young she looked. That brought on the disturbing thought that perhaps, at twenty-eight, he might be too old for her and the things he wished them to do definitely wrong. "Never."

"You're such a good dancer," she whispered. "You've mastered the waltz perfectly."

"I've heard a good dancer can lead his partner so well she can safely dance with her eyes closed," he said. "Do you believe that?"

"I've certainly never met anyone *that* good." She shook her head, making the glossy curls bounce.

"Why don't you try it now and let's see?"

"Very well." Obediently, she closed her eyes. He whirled her around again, sending her skirts sweeping the floor.

In the second turn, he exclaimed, "My dear Miss Cleary. You look pale. Are you faint?"

"Why, no." She didn't open her eyes, however. "I feel fine. How could I be pale when we're moving so quickly?"

"Nay, I think you've a bit of pallor. I believe a bit of fresh air's in order."

Deftly, Colin whirled her toward the edge of the ballroom floor. A few feet away were open doors leading to the terrace. Making certain no one was paying them heed, he swept Fiona through and outside.

She opened her eyes, looking around. "We shouldn't be here."

"Why not?" His question was so guileless it sounded false to his own ears.

"You know very well why." Unconsciously, her voice dropped to a whisper though there was no one else to hear. "If my parents see we've come out here...unchaperoned...they'll think..."

"You're right," Colin sighed, admitting his mistake. "I don't want either of them to get the wrong idea."

That was the truth. He glanced back into the ballroom. Across the floor, he saw Sir Robert's head swiveling as he looked for his daughter. He said something to Quinton. Colin's father stopped what he was saying, bowed to the man to whom he'd been speaking, and followed Sir Robert around the edge of the dance floor.

"And your father's coming this way now, so I'd better work fast."

With that, he pulled Fiona into his arms and kissed her on the lips, quickly and firmly. Then, he pushed her away.

"Whatever you do," he cautioned in a whisper. "Don't tell your father I did that."

"Wh-why not?" Fiona pressed trembling fingers to her mouth.

"Because I want to see you again, and I don't want him forbidding me the pleasure of your company."

He guided her to a nearby stone bench, whipping out his handkerchief and handing it to her. Automatically, Fiona took it. Colin seized the fan secured on her wrist by a white silken cord, pulling it free. Flipping it open, he flapped it wildly in front of her face.

Loud enough for the two men coming through the door to hear, he said, "Do you feel better now? Should I call your mother?"

"N-no, I…" Fiona looked confused. Gripping his handkerchief tightly, she pressed it to her lips. "Please, Mr. McCoy…the fan…I can barely breathe…"

She caught his wrist, stilling the rapid back-and-forth movement.

"Fiona," Sir Robert burst out. "What is this?"

"Here now, Colin, what's going on?" Quinton's question came on the heels of Sir Robert's exclamation.

"Ah, Father, Sir Robert…" Colin's expression as he turned toward both men held not the surprised guilt they expected, but concern. "I'm glad you're here, I was asking Miss Fiona if she needed her mother. She was feeling faint, and I thought perhaps the ballroom air was too stifling…" He let the rest of the sentence die away as he held up the fan, then snapped it expertly shut.

"Fiona, are you all right?" Whatever Sir Robert's previous thoughts had been, they disappeared at the suggestion his daughter might be ill.

"O-oh, yes, Father," Fiona assured him. She lowered Colin's handkerchief. "Mr. McCoy acted so quickly…" Here she gave Colin a glance that might be interpreted several ways. "I barely had a chance to feel lightheaded before we were in the fresh air and I was recovering."

"If you're ill, perhaps we should leave," Sir Robert suggested, taking his daughter's arm and guiding her back into the ballroom.

Colin, still clutching the fan, followed with Quinton behind him.

"Oh, no, please." Fiona looked across the floor to where her mother sat with the dowager baroness. "Both Mamma and Grandmamma are enjoying themselves so. I wouldn't want to spoil their evening. I assure you I'm much better now." She returned Colin's handkerchief. "Thank you, Mr. McCoy."

He accepted it, solemnly exchanging it for her fan, which she slipped back onto her wrist.

"I do think I should sit out the next couple of sets, however," Fiona continued and looked as if Colin's fallen expression pleased her. "I wouldn't want to begin dancing and again feel faint."

"Quinton...Colin, please excuse us." Sir Robert nodded to both men and guided Fiona to where his wife and mother sat. He said something and they quickly made space for her between them.

"Fresh air, Colin?" Quinton gave his son a skeptical gaze. "That old ploy?"

"Truly, sir..."

"Nay. Don't." Quinton shook his head. "I've heard that excuse an' more from your braithur."

"From Donal?"

"You know which one I mean," Quinton snapped. "I'm aware you were most circumspect while you were at university, so please don't tell me you're attemptin' followin' in Padraig's footsteps here in Tipperary."

"Sir, I assure you..."

Since the subject had been broached, Colin wanted

to again ask his father why he insisted he come back to McCoy Hall to live, for he'd never gotten a satisfactory answer. Instead, he glanced across the room, meeting Fiona's eyes.

"Me intentions toward Miss Cleary are naithin' but th' most honorable…"

Automatically falling into his father's mode of speech, he raised the handkerchief, pressing it against his lips. It held an elusive flowery scent where she'd touched it to her mouth. He felt it transfer itself to his own as if he could taste its clean sweetness. Carefully, he folded it and returned it to his pocket.

"Th' most honorable," he repeated.

Chapter 2

Colin was quiet during the coach ride home.

No one seemed to notice, however, because Felicity and his mother chattered on so, dominating whatever speech there was. Occasionally, Donal put in a word to inject a little variety into the conversation, and once or twice, Quinton spoke up, asking his wife a question about someone new he'd noticed or to make a comment on a subject Alisdaire mentioned. It was only as the horses turned through the gate and trotted down the driveway to McCoy HallHall's entrance that Quinton commented on his silence.

"You're quiet, lad. Anythin' th' matter?"

"Hm?" Colin looked around as if startled from a doze. "Oh...nay, Da. Just thinkin', that's all."

"Thinking?" Donal laughed. "We'd best be on our guard in that case. Nothing good can come of Colin thinking."

Everyone laughed, Colin joining in, if somewhat reluctantly. He was getting a wee bit tired of the jokes at his expense, especially since that was generally all his brother aimed in his direction.

"Thinking of the Honorable Fiona?" Donal, perceptive as usual, asked.

Damn. Colin wanted to clip his elder brother on the ear. "Yes, as a matter o' fact, I was." He said it like a challenge. *An' what if I am? What's it to you, big braithur?* He added, "I was wonderin' if she'd recovered from her li'l indisposition. I noticed she didn't dance any more but sat beside her grandma th' rest o' th' time."

"Couldn't have been much of an indisposition," Quinton commented. "She ate rather heartily o' th' li'l cakes at th' buffet, an' drank several cups o' punch, too."

So, Da had been watching her. Colin wondered if *he* also had been under surveillance the rest of the evening. He was glad he hadn't done anything overt during that time.

"That was quick thinking," his mother commented.

Her own gentle lilt was in contrast to her husband's more harsh tones, or perhaps, after hearing Lord Robert and his daughter speak tonight, Colin was simply abruptly more sensitive to accents. He gave his mother a questioning look.

"Taking her outside like that when she went faint," she explained. "I imagine you saved her from a most embarrassing moment."

"Oh, he certainly did," Donal spoke up with a catch in his voice that was almost a snort. "Good thinking, little brother."

"Thank you, Mama," Colin answered. He speared Donal with a gaze barely visible in the dim light of the coach. "An' thank you for noticin', braithur."

Donal smirked and Colin fell silent.

They were at the manor house now. The driver brought the horses to a stop and they stood stamping and snorting as the footman leaped down and opened the door, pulling down the steps so his father could alight. Quinton waited while he assisted Màiri-Caitlin and then Felicity from the coach, and stood aside for Colin and his brother. Once they were standing beside it, the footman collapsed the steps, closed the door and climbed back to his perch.

"Shall I stable th' horses an' put th' coach away, sir?" the driver asked.

Quinton nodded. "No one'll be goin' back out t'night."

With the footman clinging to the safety straps, the coachman gathered the reins, cracked his whip, and drove the coach around the manor to the stables located at the back of the house.

Inside, Quinton dismissed the servants who'd waited up, telling the butler to lock up. As this was done, he and Donal retired to Quinton's study while Màiri and Felicity pleaded exhaustion and climbed the stairs to their bedrooms. Colin politely excused himself from joining his brother and father. Since he was definitely now of age, it was his privilege to stay up with them and have a late night brandy if he chose.

"A bit tired, Da," he stated. "All that dancin', I suppose. Th' excitement o' it all fair wore me out." He cocked his head to one side as if thinking. "Do you suppose th' lasses feel this way, too?"

Without waiting for an answer, he started up the stairs.

Quinton hadn't shut the study door. He set about serving himself and Donal. Colin could hear the muffled *pop* of the glass stopper being removed from the brandy decanter and the sound of liquid being poured. There was more movement as the decanter was replaced and the two men took their seats on either side of the hearth, though it was still too warm for a fire to be lit.

"Will you be sleepin' in your own bed t'night?" Quinton's question floated through the study door and up the stairs to Colin.

It was a casual sounding question but at the same time such an intrusive one, especially for a father to ask a married son. That made Colin pause.

"Isn't that a rather personal question?" Donal apparently thought so, too, though he tempered the sharpness of his reply with, "Where else would I sleep, sir?"

"In your wife's, perhaps?"

"Father, you aren't going to start that again, are you?" The whine in Donal's voice was unmistakable, as well as surprising.

Well now, this may get interestin'. Colin had never heard that tone in his brother's voice before. It was that of a child who thought he'd been reprimanded unfairly.

"You've been married quite some time now, Donal, an' I've yet t' be given th' happy news that Felicity's with child." There was a pause while Quinton took a sip of his brandy. "Why haven't I?"

"Really, sir. Must you ask that?" Donal sounded completely affronted.

Shrugging, Colin resumed his trudge up the stairs. He had no desire to listen to his father berate his brother for something he himself felt couldn't be planned like a breakfast menu or an architect's blueprint. He remembered when Quinton wrote Donal practically giving him an order to marry.

Lord, that seems a long time ago now, though it's been less than a dozen years.

"I'm afraid I must." Quinton sounded completely unsympathetic to any embarrassment he was causing his son. "I arranged t' pay off that dollymop you dabbed. She swore she was knapped with your babe, so I know there's no reason you can't sire a legitimate one." There was a slight pause. "Unless she lied?"

Colin nearly tripped on the stair and paused, clutching the railing. Donal? Mr. Staid and Dry-As-Dust since his marriage…with a lovechild? *Well!* If Quinton had been speaking of Padraig, he wouldn't have been surprised at all. *But Donal…?*

Colin was shocked. He wondered when it happened. He thought he'd been aware of his brother's actions while they were at university.

"Sometimes these things take time," Donal hedged.

Colin noticed he didn't answer Quinton's question.

"Not usually." It was apparent Quinton wasn't going to take that excuse. "You were born a year after your maithur an' I were wed…an' Padraig a year after that, an' Bridget eighteen months later, an' Colin…"

"Please, I don't need to be reminded of the birthdates of my siblings." This time, Donal didn't hide his irritation.

"Whene'er you're in this house, you never visit your wife o' an evening."

"Do you listen outside my door?" Donal's tone went icy.

"Not exactly," Quinton denied. "But there's a board in the floor in front o' th' door t' Felicity's room that creaks when stepped upon. It's been silent so far."

"So, you *have* been listening! God, my own father…spying on me."

Colin imagined Donal rolling his eyes and glancing heavenward.

"'Twasn't spyin'," Quinton denied. "I've simply had trouble sleepin' lately an'…"

"The truth is, Father, I didn't think it would be

proper for Felicity and myself to…uh…not in my parents' home."

"Not proper? Codswallop! Your presence here doesn't stop your maithur an' me from…ne'er mind that." Quinton sighed. "Donal, you're me heir an' therefore you must give me a grandchild. Am I goin' t' have t' find your bastard an' legitimize it so th' McCoy name can continue?"

There was movement as Donal got to his feet. He must've gulped down the rest of his brandy for there was a quick inhalation and a sharp cough before the sound of the goblet being placed upon a table.

Footsteps coming toward the open door made Colin realized he was going to be caught leaning against the banister in the pose of an eavesdropper. He dashed up the stairs as noiselessly as possible, taking them two at a time. Reaching the second story, he disappeared around the curve of the hallway leading to the bedchambers as Donal shut the door.

****

Colin's manservant was waiting for him. He opened the door, stepping back to allow the young master to enter.

"Did you have a pleasant evenin', sir?" He followed Colin inside.

"Passable enough, I suppose." Colin decided to hold his feelings about Fiona Cleary close to his heart, not even sharing them with Geoffrey, who had become the keeper of many secrets since Quinton hired the young man to attend his son when Colin turned sixteen.

Geoffrey had been a bare year older, son of Quinton's own valet, and he was not only manservant but also confidante, sympathizer, and companion ever since. He'd been left behind when Colin went away to school, Quinton of the opinion a student didn't need a valet because selecting and caring for his clothing and running his own errands would be good for his son, teaching him responsibility.

Even after the other boys were allowed to bring their own servants to school and set themselves up in bachelor digs off-campus, Colin suffered the embarrassment of not only having no valet but of becoming his older brother's fag. He didn't realize Donal had pulled a few strings to make that happen, to prevent his younger brother from being mistreated by a malicious and prejudiced senior because of his pronounced Irish accent.

Colin also wasn't aware how, when he first came to Eton, Donal had been hazed because of his own speech. A tally stick had been hung around his neck, marks made on it every time he mispronounced a word or spoke Irish slang. The number of marks decided whether Donal got privileges along with the others boys. He learned quickly enough and within a month lost his accent completely. Now he spoke with the *received pronunciation* of a well-educated Irishman, namely like an Englishman.

Donal didn't want that mistreatment for Colin but neither did he want it said he was coddling his baby brother. Colin's adjusting his accent to whomever he was talking to irritated Donal while conversely making him proud the boy had found his own solution to that problem.

It was only after Colin returned to Tipperary permanently that he and his valet were reunited. By that time, Colin had a great respect for the tedious work a valet had to do, after having been more or less his brother's manservant for an entire year before Donal graduated.

Colin pulled loose his cravat as he spoke, with one tug completely obliterating the beauty of Geoffrey's masterpiece. He held it out and the valet caught it as it slid from his hand. Geoffrey placed it on the arm of a nearby chair and proceeded to pull the evening coat from Colin's shoulders as his master turned his back and raised his arms slightly.

The coat and vest followed the neckpiece to the chair. Colin toed off his evening slippers. In stocking feet, he stalked to the turned-down bed. It looked as puffy as a cloud, and just as soft and inviting.

A startling image of Fiona Cleary, clad in something lacy and frothy, superimposed itself upon the pillows.

Colin stopped, blinked, and rubbed his eyes. He stared at the pillows. Nothing there but the white Egyptian cotton cases, each embroidered with the McCoy crest.

Lord, I must be more tired than I thought. He certainly hadn't had enough spiked punch to cause him to see things. He decided he needed to think about that vision.

"I'm not going t' sleep for a while," he said aloud, suddenly wanting to be alone. "Just get out me nightshirt an' lay it on th' bed. I'll finish undressin' by meself."

"Yes, sir." Opening the free-standing wardrobe, Geoffrey carefully placed the evening jacket in it. He brought out a white sleeping shirt and laid it across the foot of the bed. With a bow, he went out, taking the cravat and vest with him to be cleaned and ironed. He shut the door behind him.

Colin stared at the door a moment, then pulled his shirt over his head, tossing it to the now-empty chair. He unbuttoned his evening trousers, reflecting he should've had Geoffrey stay and help him finish undressing. *Now there'll be more work for him tomorrow and things'll be wrinkled because they weren't hung up tonight.*

Colin could've done that chore himself but that was Geoffrey's job, and it would be wrong for him to do something assigned to another, especially since the valet was being paid for the chore. In a brief moment of brotherly expansiveness, Donal had taught Colin that. Also, the memory of all the times he'd hung up Donal's clothing still clung, and he'd sworn, once he was freed of his brother's servitude, he'd never do that again.

Stockings followed, and he picked up the nightshirt, shaking it out and studying it a moment. For something worn only in the privacy of his bedchamber, it was as elaborate as his evening shirt, with heavy smocking on the yoke and down each sleeve, ending in a loose cuff. The body of the shirt was plain except for a buttoned placket dividing the yoke at the neck, and halfway down a hemmed and reinforced split in the fabric. The first time Colin saw that opening in a nightshirt, he'd wondered what it was for. He wasn't curious enough to ask anyone, however, deciding it was for easy access to piss. He always thought that odd, however, since hiking up the nightshirt was an easier way to give the ol' Percy its freedom to do what had to be done.

That led to another delicious image of Fiona Cleary and himself, and this one was so forbidden he squelched it in mid-thought before it could go further.

Hurriedly, he slid the nightshirt over his head. As he did so, he caught sight of himself in the cheval glass near the wardrobe. Colin stopped, shirt still clutched in his hands and wrapped around his shoulders. He studied his image, turning his back slightly.

Hm. Bum looks pretty good. Tight, anyways. He twisted, giving attention to his drumsticks. Pretty thin but definitely long. Long legs were a McCoy trait...*those thighs need more muscle*...and his chest...*it was wide enough but*...his ribs were still slightly prominent.

He remembered how stick-thin Donal looked when he was twenty-two, His brother had mourned loudly his lack of breadth while Quinton brushed his worries aside.

You'll fill out, lad. Just give yourself time. After all, you're barely an adult.

Sure enough, a few years later, Donal was as hefty and sturdy as his father.

Colin hoped he'd be the same way. He studied his chest a moment longer, then allowed his gaze to slide downward. *As for that...* He stared at the pale organ in its wiry nest.

"Damn, looks like 'tis surrounded by copper baccapipes!" Still, 'twas good for what it was made for, he supposed. At least the few women he'd graced with it hadn't complained.

He let the nightshirt drop, spun and climbed into bed. Turning down the lamp, he settled himself upon the pillows. He wanted to think, needed to...of Fiona Cleary, and what he was going to do about the way she made him feel.

Fiona. Just thinking about her made a warm glow encircle his heart. It didn't stop there, however, but grew until his entire body was filled with heat, swirling, converging, and centering itself directly on his rod. It promptly twitched.

"None o' that now." Colin laid a hand on the organ. It seemed to argue it wasn't time to rest but that it and its owner should stay awake a bit longer. "That's what I'm tryin' t' do," he said and laughed. "What am I doin'? Talking t' me Percy? What I need t' do is *think*."

He settled himself a little deeper into the pillows, closed his eyes, and forced himself to concentrate on something other than the tingling between his legs.

****

Colin had lost his virginity shortly after his second term at Eton. Donal saw to that during one of the few times he'd taken his younger brother under his wing and wasn't ordering him about. Padraig was gone from the school by then, though his reputation lingered, despite his physical presence no longer being there.

Promising his father he wouldn't allow the baby of the family to be led down all the wicked paths their brother had traveled, Donal kept an eye on Colin.

Nevertheless, he made certain baby brother was introduced to a few of those paths, urging moderation in any acquired vices. Colin accompanied Donal and some of his chums to various ale houses and other places frequented by students.

One night, they'd been accosted on a street corner by a ladybird who had eyes on Colin though she offered to dab both of them for a sum, shocking Donal with its low price. If he'd been alone, he might've taken her up on it, but he turned her away, dragging a loudly protesting Colin from the spot.

"Very well," Donal snapped. "If you in that much of a hurry to get yourself shucked, we'll do it properly."

With that, he hailed a passing cab, and shoved Colin inside.

"Where are we going?" Colin asked.

"To have an act performed that apparently is

becoming necessary." Donal sighed. "Let's get it out of the way so it won't become a future obstacle."

"What?" Colin looked as if he didn't understand.

Donal said to the cabbie, "We need to go to some place where we can relieve our tensions."

The man nodded, snapped his whip, and the horse started off at a smart trot.

"Donal, I really don't want t' go t' anaithur club…" Colin's thoughts were still on the dolly and what he considered a lost opportunity. He fell silent as his brother waved his protests away.

"Sit there and be quiet."

When the cab pulled up in front of a slightly shabby-looking white brick building on the edge of town, Donal paid the driver, got out and pulled Colin from the vehicle. He went up the steps and rapped on the door.

It swung open.

A woman stood in the doorway. She was dressed in a richly brocaded gown, similar to one Colin remembered his mother owning. This one seemed overdone, however. It was too rich, too splendid, the ornamentation too lavish and elaborate, the color too bright and gaudy. The woman herself was overblown with round full breasts overflowing the bosom of the gown while her figure stopped just short of being plump. Her hair was a mass of curls and ringlets, piled high on her head and the most impossible shade of red, a flame color even brighter than either Colin or Donal's own hair.

"Well now." When she spoke, her voice matched the rest of her, full, soft, and overdone. "If it ain't Mr. Donal. Welcome back, luv." She released the door, throwing her arms around Donal and kissing him on the lips so loudly that Colin, standing behind him, heard the *smack* clearly.

While Colin gaped in shock, Donal returned the kiss quite enthusiastically.

He couldn't believe it. His brother...kissing someone voluntarily. He remembered how Donal always shied from kissing his aunts and girl cousins, once actually wiping his lips after a great-aunt waylaid him and pressed her mouth to his. He was always so reserved and polite, usually icily so, around females, but now...

That was the moment Colin learned about duplicity and that his brother carefully hid his more earthy feelings behind a staid and well-controlled exterior.

He stood with his mouth open in surprise.

The woman released Donal, saw Colin and asked, "And who's this little doll baby?"

Donal caught Colin's arm, drawing him forward. The boy moved reluctantly, still stunned by seeing his brother acting so wantonly. "This is my brother, Colin."

"Please to meet you, Mr. Colin," the woman said. "Welcome."

Colin actually winced.

"He's come for some instruction," Donal supplied. "And introduction."

"Ah, I see." The woman winked. "This is the place for it, then." Catching Colin's arm, she gestured. "There they are, lad...take your pick."

Colin continued to stare and not speak. The movement of her hand brought his attention to a row of couches filled with women, packed so tightly some of them were almost sitting in each other's laps. They were naked or mostly so, merely wearing sheer, ruffled wrappers fastened at the waist and leaving little to the imagination...and Colin had always thought he had a very fanciful imagination.

"I…uh…I…" he finally managed to mumble. The madam moved slightly, making impatient motions. He raised a hand, realized it was shaking, and pointed to a girl with hair of the palest shade of blonde he'd ever seen. "Her?"

He let the hand drop.

"Good choice." The madam clapped him on the back, making him stagger as she beckoned to the girl. "You, Sadie…get yourself over here and take Mr. Colin upstairs."

The girl extracted herself from under the naked thighs of the one seated next to her and strolled over, not hurrying in the least. Her hips rolled smoothly as she walked, as though a ball-bearing were caught between them.

Colin goggled. Donal hid a smirk.

The madam caught the girl by the arm, lowering her head and voice to whisper, "He's new, so do him up right and make a veteran of him."

Sadie nodded, hooked her arm through Colin's, and guided him toward the stairs.

"Did I hear your name's Colin?" She had a low husky voice, sending chills down his core directly to his groin. "That's a lovely name. One of my favorites." She pushed back one of the curls hanging over his eyes. "Red hair. You have to be Donnie's brother."

Donnie? Colin started to speak, coughed, and managed, "Aye, that I am." He knew he was acting like the virgin he was. That caused him to flush, only making it worse.

"Don't be nervous." She leaned closer, nuzzling against his neck, laughing as the warmth of her breath tickled his skin and he shivered. "By the time we're finished, you'll be able to give Donnie a run for his money where dabbing's concerned."

Colin swallowed loudly. "Do you think so?" That sounded both hopeful and stupid but at the moment, his mind seemed to have stopped working.

"Sweetheart…"

His nervousness amused her. She caught his hand, pressing it against her breast and when he tried to pull away, wrapped her fingers around his, forcing them to close on the nipple. Colin took a deep breath, letting his fingers tighten of their own accord.

"I know so."

He was wildly aware of Donal and the madam watching, of other eyes looking up at them, everyone seemed to be glancing his way.

He had a sudden desire to give them a show, make Donal envious and perhaps a little proud of his baby brother. His fingers stroked that lush breast. He lowered his head, kissing the nipple and biting at it delicately before sucking it into his mouth. Sadie leaned against him and practically purred.

"That's the way to do it." She pulled away, starting up the stairs. "Come on."

He stumbled along with her eagerly.

She led Colin to a nearby door. Inside, there was a bed and nothing else but a wash stand. The bed had a single surprisingly clean sheet and thick draperies, two pillows, and that was all.

Before he realized it, Sadie had him out of his clothing, nodding approvingly at what she saw. Colin took a deep breath and reached for her. She dodged, lifting the ironstone pitcher on the washstand. While he watched, she poured water into a basin and brought it to where he stood.

"Wh-what' s that for?" he dared asked.

"Your nebuchadnezzar there's looking a bit weak." She nodded downward.

Automatically, he put up a hand, shielding his member and thinking how pale and limp it appeared. What happened? It had been so ready when the dollymop stopped them.

"I thought a bit of a bath might restore his vigor."

Colin didn't know what to say to that so he stood still as she set the basin on the bed, wrung out the cloth in the water, and reached for him. He shivered as the warmth of her hand closed around his shaft. When she pressed the cloth to his flesh, however, he flinched.

"It's cold." The words jerked from him.

"Oh? Sorry." She dropped the cloth back into the water and bent, breathing gently against his damp flesh, blowing heated little puffs of air while her hands clasped and cradled.

That lasted about four seconds.

"I think I'm warm enough, thank you." Colin put his arms around her and swung both of them onto the bed, knocking the basin to the floor. It struck and bounced, sending water spraying.

That had been his introduction to the carnal side of life, compliments of his older brother. Later, Colin learned Padraig had also been a patron at the same house, finding the place on his own. That McCoy son was still spoken of with longing by some of the girls.

Now considering himself as adult as everyone else, Colin was eager for a return trip. Visits were costly, however, and would be at his own expense, Donal informed him as they stood outside and he hailed a cab for their ride back to school.

Colin soon depleted his allowance, and set to saving future ones then and there. He realized it was going to be a long time before the next visit because he had other necessities he had to buy out of the stipend Quinton sent him. Using it up so quickly might warrant explanations he wasn't prepared to give his father.

Lack of money didn't prevent primal urges, however.

One night when he and his roommate Phelan were having a pint at the snug most of their group patronized, he found himself attracted to the barmaid's charms. Abruptly hot and randy, he asked her if she'd was interested in a bit of dab. Setting down her tray, she led him to a small room off the hallway behind the bar, where she leaned against the wall and lifted her skirts.

She was bare beneath and the dark thatch at the apex of her thighs was the most arousing thing he'd seen. He remembered Sadie's shaved cunny and how that had excited him, too.

Hell, seein' a woman in any condition sends me Percy risin', he decided. He put his arms around her. She pushed him away and held out her hand.

"Coin first."

Dropping the money into her hand, he pushed her against the wall while he unbuttoned his trousers with his other hand.

When they returned to the table where Phelan was patiently waiting, the girl nodded to his friend, said, "Sorry to leave you alone so long, luv," and took him by the hand.

Colin wondered why he didn't feel the least bit of

jealousy as she led Phelan down the hallway also.

Later, when he mentioned this to Donal, his brother reacted so furiously, Colin was momentarily frightened.

"You idiot. Haven't you more sense than to let yourself get fucked by some tavern wench?" He shook his head, voice rising in exasperation. "Next to forking a street bird, that's the best way to get the pox or the glim or something else as deadly."

A hand went to Colin's shoulder, shaking him slightly.

"Col, promise me you won't do that again. If you get the urge, just hail a cab, tell the driver what I did that night. They all know what it means."

"But, Donal…I can't afford…"

That was as far as he got.

"If you get that desperate, I'll lend you the money." That, coming from Donal, who was generally as tight with his own allowance as a Scot, shook Colin, for it proved how serious his brother was about his younger sibling's sexual welfare. "If it'll keep you safe. Promise me that, will you, Col?"

He shook Colin's shoulder again in emphasis.

"All right, Donal," Colin nodded. "I promise."

"Good. Now then." Donal released him. "Watch your prick for the next month. If it turns red, you get a rash, or even a pimple, tell me. I know a doctor who's discreet."

That really frightened Colin, so much in fact, as soon as he got back to his room, he stripped and began to examine his nether flesh.

"Good God, Colin!"

Rod clutched in his hand, he froze, looking up to see Phelan standing in the doorway. His roommate hurried in, slamming the door.

"If you're going to pull your Percy, the least you can do is lock the door first."

"I'm not...doin' that," Colin replied. "I'm checkin'."

"For what?" Phelan sat down on his bed, carefully looking everywhere except at him.

"For signs o' th' pox." He told Phelan what Donal said.

"Oh God. I plowed her, too," Phelan reminded him.

"Then you'd better give yourself a look."

"Right." Running to the door, Phelan locked it. "Wouldn't do for one of the proctors to walk in here and see us both with our pricks in our hands. They'd be certain we're mandrakes."

In the next four weeks, both anxiously and faithfully repeated this examination each night, finding nothing, and relaxing with relief.

Twice more in that year, Colin was loaned money by Donal. In between and afterward, he kept himself busy with his studies, earning good grades in return for stifled sexual urges. He told himself it was best that way, to stay relatively chaste rather than risk involvement with some dire disease. Phelan followed his example and they were healthy if not exactly happy.

Much later, after his graduation from Eton and before entering Cambridge, Colin came to London for a visit. At that time, Donal was courting Felicity, balancing seeing her with hurried trips to his mistress, as he attempted to convince himself he wasn't actually falling in love. That was shortly after Colin learned of Padraig's banishment. He'd gone to his elder brother, hoping for comfort and some diversion to ease the shock, as well as assuage an abruptly awakening carnal urge.

Colin got more than he bargained for. Donal obliged by taking him to the most notorious place of its kind in the city, a toss-house where no one ventured except in disguise, if he wanted to keep his reputation intact while indulging his physical side.

It was called the Church, the madam the Abbess, and Colin and his brother definitely worshipped heavily that night.

Going there had been an education as well as an experience.

Colin marveled how Donal managed to hide his predilections under such a controlled, dignified exterior, and also wondered why Padraig never tried to blackmail him with the knowledge. He was certain his other brother was aware. Nothing much got past Padraig.

After leaving Cambridge, Colin followed the general course, a tour of the continent, the event usually celebrating a young man's entry into the adult world, except Quinton didn't trust him to go alone. Colin suffered the humiliation of being chaperoned by his father as he visited the capital cities of Europe. The completion of his education was attained while any dalliances Colin hopefully planned were circumvented by Quinton's presence.

Upon their return to Ireland, the youngster was further confounded to learn his father wished him to live at home.

Colin protested but Quinton made it sound so logical. Donal now had a wife so he couldn't be expected to live with his brother. Padraig was now somewhere in America, doing who knew what. Quinton needed a son at home, to aid him in running his own estate as well as acting in Lord Alisdaire's behalf, and Colin was chosen.

That's the way the youngest McCoy son's life ran until the night of the Tipperary ball and he met Fiona Cleary.

****

Colin thought of Fiona and how it felt as his lips touched hers, the brief press of her body against his…he was certain he'd felt the hard little points of her breasts against his waistcoat as he hugged her. Surely the girl had been as excited as he. That sent a single stab of desire through him.

Colin me lad, 'tis goin' t' be a severe trial for you but you can do it, he told himself. *There'll be no goin' t' Church here, unless 'tis t' th' real thing for confession.*

Chapter 3

Colin awoke with the intense sensation there was something he needed to do but he had no idea what. It was such a sense of a need for eminent action that he lay there, concentrating heavily, trying to determine the reason he felt that way. That was why, though he was generally an early riser, he was still abed when Geoffrey's discreet knock broke the silence.

Given permission to enter, the valet appeared surprised, then concerned to see him still lying in bed. "Sir, are you ill?"

It always made Colin smile when Geoffrey got formal and spoke to him as servant to master.

"Shall I ask Mr. Cormac t' fetch a doctor?" Geoffrey hovered at the bedside as if Colin were in his last throes.

That made him laugh. "Nay, I'm fine…just had a bit t' think on an' didn't want t' stir until I'd thought it through."

Colin sat up and threw back the covers.

"Did you get it thought out?" Geoffrey reverted to their usual conversational mode, that of friends.

"Nay." Colin stood up. "Goin' t' take more than a few minutes rumination, I imagine." He shook his head as if that would toss out the thoughts whirling inside it. "Well, now. May as well prepare t' greet th' day. What do you suggest I wear?"

****

42

Breakfast was a mostly silent affair. Quinton had already taken his meal and gone, riding out on errands and to visit various tenants who'd sent him notifications they needed aid or wished to confer with him. It was unusual that Quinton always went to the tenants. They never came to him, as most other stewards expected tenants to do. That was probably one of the reasons the people liked him so and kept any discontent to a minimum, because they didn't want him replaced by someone unsympathetic.

Donal was at table and that didn't make Colin feel a bit better. Though Felicity smiled at him, his brother didn't look up as he entered, so Colin didn't speak but simply stalked to the sideboard and applied himself to inspecting the dishes.

A footman hurried to Colin's side, picking up one of the plates set on the end of the buffet counter. He unwrapped it from its warming cloths and waiting expectantly for Colin to make his choices. There was enough to hold his attention for several minutes…hot toast and muffins in stacked dishes, heated to keep their contents warm, three bowls of jam, chafing dishes with butter-fried potatoes and onions, hard-whipped eggs cooked with chives, links of sausage, and something appearing to be a bright red fish that had been butterflied and jugged. Set in the center of each portion was a symmetrically rounded but soft-fried egg.

Donal turned his attention from his own meal to notice his brother's indecision. "It's herring…kippered herring," he explained.

"A fish? For breakfast?" Colin was well aware what kippers were and also that in England, they were an accepted part of the first meal of the day. He'd simply never seen any on the McCoy buffet before, so pretended ignorance. "Why?"

"I'm afraid that's my fault," Felicity spoke up. "I do love them so and I asked Donal to request the cook prepare some." She smiled at her husband. "So, he did."

"Hm." That was all Colin could say.

If Donal admitted wanting the things, he'd have gibed him some, but since it was Felicity…

"I'll give it a try," he decided. "But I prefer me eggs with chives." He glanced at his sister-in-law. "Is it permissible if I remove this egg an' replace it with anaithur?"

"I don't see why not."

She looked pleased he was going to partake of her favorite breakfast repast.

Colin hurried through the other items, pointing to this one, selecting a portion of that, and the footman carefully placed each on his plate. He turned to the table, the footman setting the plate before him, then pushing in his chair as Colin sat.

"You like them, too?" He nodded at Donal's plate where a whole herring lay, as yet untouched, though his brother was tucking into the potatoes and onions quite enthusiastically.

"Of course." Donal didn't look up. "We have them several times a week at home…I mean, in London."

Colin let that little slip go. After the exchange he'd heard last night, he wasn't going to say anything that might upset Felicity. He had a sudden sympathy for his sister-in-law, and a startling wonder if Donal really loved her, if he avoided her bed in London also. If that was the case, his brother was a superb actor, for he appeared not only loving but protective of his wife.

That made him think of the Church and a curiosity if his brother still went there now that he had a spouse. He remembered his own visit and the frantic bouts of lust his younger self had unleashed. Perhaps Donal preferred that to the quietly dutiful relations he had with his wife. At least Colin imagined them to be quiet. He really couldn't envision well-mannered little Felicity rolling about in carnal abandon.

A sudden flush to his face made him push that thought from his mind. It was no business of his what his brother and his wife did in the privacy of their bedchamber last night, or any other night for that matter. Remembering what Quinton said, Colin had listened for the creak of that specific board and felt a sudden satisfaction when he heard it before he fell asleep.

"Why are they red?" He got his mind back to breakfast.

"It's the way they're prepared," Felicity explained before Donal could answer.

That surprised Colin, who'd found her to be relatively quiet most of the time. Last night in the coach had been an exception.

"They're salted or pickled, then cold-smoked. The method of curing is what makes them red." She nodded at the fish on Colin's plate, then ate more of her own. "These have been jugged, by the way."

"Aye, I figured that, since they're whole." He made no move to sample it, however.

Felicity laid down her fork and dabbed her lips with her napkin. "If you'll excuse me, Donal…Colin…I'm going with Mother Màiri into one of the villages today. For a charity visit."

Dropping her napkin by her plate, she got to her feet.

A footman pulled back her chair. Felicity started to move away.

"Wait." Donal stood also.

When she hesitated, he leaned over and pressed a kiss to her cheek. "I shall miss you. Hurry back."

She blushed, nodded, and hurried away. The footman pushed the chair back under the table and resumed his place. A second footman stepped forward and removed the plate, carrying it to the kitchen. Donal again sat and applied himself to his breakfast.

"You made it appear you love her," Colin commented, biting into a heavily buttered crumpet. The crust was crisp and he crunched noisily.

"I do." Donal didn't rise to the bait but made a simple statement and continued eating.

"Really?" Colin set down the remnants of the crumpet and stared at his brother.

"I suppose it may be difficult for you to understand." Donal set down his fork and gave his younger brother his attention.

For the first time, Colin saw that he looked tired, as if he'd gotten little sleep last night. He hoped that lack of sleep was going to be productive.

"I love my wife."

"You're right," Colin agreed. "I don't understand. After all I learned at school about you, an' later, I'd have thought you wouldn't even glance at such a well-bred li'l thin'."

"You'll keep quiet about my schooldays, and any part of my life of which you have knowledge, little brother." Donal's reply was spoken softly but his tone was as sharp as a whip cut. "What I did at Eton or Cambridge or any other place stays there. Not even

Father is aware of some of it and certainly not Felicity. I wish it to stay that way." He paused, giving Colin a harsh gaze. "Do you understand?"

"Of course, Donal." A little shaken by this show of emotion as well as the underlying threat, Colin nodded. "Mum's th' word."

"I don't want Felicity embarrassed...or hurt...because she's heard of something I did before we met," Donal continued. His voice underwent a change, becoming earnest. "I do love her. She's sweet, intelligent, and pretty. Besides, we share enough of the same interests to have a harmonious life."

"That's important? Sharing the same interests?" Colin was surprised at the revelations his brother was making. At the breakfast table, too.

"Very."

Colin decided to risk asking. "So, you don't go t' Church anymore?"

"Never." Donal didn't look at him but picked up his toast and bit into it. He chewed, swallowed, and then said, very quietly, "I don't miss that form of worship at all. I'll be indiscreet and say Felicity gives me enough passion in private to eclipse any of that congregation."

That surprised Colin so he didn't know what to say, deciding it was best not to say anything. He was saved the problem of a reply as Donal glanced at the kipper, then at a footman and said, "Take this away. Feed it to one of the stable cats, and bring me some eggs and chives."

As the man obeyed, Colin asked, "You're not eatin' it? I thought you liked..."

"Can't stand the things," Donal admitted briskly. "Only eat them because Felicity likes them...and I eat as little as possible." He thanked the footman for the plate piled high with eggs cooked delicately with chives and a generous helping of white pepper, lifted his fork and stabbed into the mixture with relish. "It doesn't hurt to make small sacrifices like eating a kipper if it makes her happy."

Colin made a valiant effort to eat part of his. He picked at it, cut off a bit with his fork and tasted it, then swallowed manfully and shook his head. "The cats will have a feast this morning." He waved away his own plate, and one of the footmen hastily removed it. "Bring me some potatoes, a muffin, an' that raspberry jam bowl."

"Been meaning to tell you…" Donal looked up as Colin began to smear jam onto his muffin. "I commend you on your fast thinking regarding Lord Alisdaire's daughter last night."

"Oh? I wasn't aware you were watchin'." Colin bit into the muffin.

"Brother, where you're concerned, I'm always on the lookout." Briefly, there was a glint of humor in Donal's green eyes. It faded as he became serious. "Be careful, Colin. Don't do anything to jeopardize Father's position with Alisdaire."

"Wouldn't think o' it," Colin assured him. "Matter o' fact…an' I told Da this last night…I have nothin' but th' most honorable intentions where Miss Cleary is concerned."

"God, that sounds serious." Donal stopped eating, fork in midair, staring at him.

"I fear it may be," Colin admitted. He swallowed the last bite of muffin and sat, hands on either side of his plate. "Donal, how does it feel to be in love?"

"I can't answer that question. I'm afraid my definition of that emotion might not coincide with yours."

"All right then," Colin tried again. "How did you know Felicity was th' one you wished t' marry?"

"I imagine you'll consider it coldblooded," Donal answered. "When I accepted it was my duty to marry, I made a list of the eligible young ladies I was attracted to, called upon each to determine with which one I had the most compatibility and a majority of the same interests. Then I concentrated on that one long enough to realize being daily and nightly in her company wouldn't be a strain on my nerves because I actually was forming a fondness for her."

"God, when you put it like that, it does sound coldblooded, heartless even," Colin exclaimed.

"That's why I believe we should draw this particular conversation to a close." Donal spoke abruptly, his stiff manner returning, becoming once more British and no longer the teasing big brother he'd been before he went away to school. "You're too much of a romantic to be realistic about certain phases of life."

He glanced at the clock over the mantel of the dining room fireplace.

"It's getting late, nearly eight, and I've some correspondence I need to tend. Can't let things in London come to a standstill simply because I'm visiting my parents for an extended stay."

Donal was now in business with Felicity's uncle, a shipping merchant.

"Nay," Colin agreed, feeling the loss of that old camaraderie, as brief as it had been. "We wouldn't want that, would we?"

Donal didn't reply. He simply finished his breakfast and left. Colin followed him a few moments later. Amid the clatter of dishes while the footmen and maids cleared the table as well as the buffet, he told Cormac, "Have a groom saddle one of me horses an' bring him 'round."

Sometime during his conversation with his brother, he realized he had to see Fiona Cleary again. That day. He returned to his room to change to riding clothes.

Chapter 4

Colin was on the road to Alisdaire Manor before he realized it. *What the hell am I doin'? About t' commit mesef' t' somethin' I'm not e'en certain I want, that's what.*

He couldn't get Fiona Cleary's pretty face out of his mind. He thought of what Donal had said and envisioned any young woman he'd met with whom he'd shown the slightest interest.

Colin always behaved circumspectly around the daughters of his friends as well as any he'd been introduced to while at school, unconsciously trying to make reparation for Padraig's behavior. With none of them had he felt any emotion as he had with Fiona, however, and he'd certainly never whisked one away for even the briefest kiss. He'd never acted in any way that might be considered compromising where any of them were concerned.

So, why with Fiona Cleary?

Truly, if their fathers had appeared a few seconds earlier and found them in that embrace…he shuddered to think what Alisdaire or Quinton might've done.

He was nearing the great stone gates through which the driveway led to the manor courtyard. It was cobbled and his horse's hooves made a sharp clip-clop as it picked its way.

The manor house was a magnificent edifice, making

McCoy Hall, with its thirty bedrooms, seem small in comparison. Even in sunlight it loomed high and dark before them. It was a typical sixteenth-century affair, a bastardized Inigo Jones design one of the late Lords Alisdaire had ordered copied and transported to Tipperary. There were gables and strap work and other architectural niceties transforming the large stone building sprawling before them. It had several stories and twice that many windows reflecting the sun.

The front was bordered with wide beds of flowers, ablaze with color in the morning sunshine. Colin wondered if Fiona had any say in what was planted there, then decided the flowers, or their ancestors, had probably been set long before she was born.

In our garden, she'll choose th' plantin' o' all th' flowers. Where had that thought come from?

To one side of the door stood a painted metal post with a rounded top, a hitching ring through it. On the stoop, a youngster was seated on a stool. Doubtless some groom's son, or an apprentice stable boy, for he leaped up, reaching for the bit as Colin stopped his horse.

"Don't bother," Colin told him. "I'll just tie him here. I daresay I won't be long."

The boy nodded and returned to his place and Colin went up the stoop to the door.

He studied the knocker, an ornate, brass thing with a horseshoe-shaped flange. Seizing it, he brought it down against the metal plate three times, with a steady, knolling *thud*. The echo of the last strike had barely died away when he heard footsteps inside.

There was the click of a lock and the door swung open.

"Yes, sir?" A very dignified man stood there, silver-haired, dressed in the dark blue of what Colin imagined was Lord Alisdaire's livery. "May I help you?"

"Good morning." Colin swallowed, cleared his throat and adjusted his speech. "Mr. Colin McCoy to see His Lordship if he's receiving."

He was abruptly aware of the stable boy watching him and thought the butler's gaze was amused.

"Of course." The man nodded. "Do you have a card, sir?"

Card? Colin felt a moment's panic. Had he brought his calling cards with him?

Though he'd apparently known subconsciously what he was going to do since the moment he awoke, he couldn't remember if he had. He thrust a hand into an inside breast pocket, felt the little gold case, and brought it out. Geoffrey, bless him, when he assisted him in dressing… He remembered the valet's hand going to the inside of his jacket a moment. He'd merely thought he was smoothing the lining.

Flipping open the case, he selected a card and placed it on the little silver tray the butler held out. *Coilin Uilliam Conchobhar McCoy, Esquire*, it read in elegant black-inked script, *McCoy Dúiche,* again his father's affectation of their heritage, written in Gaillich, on the finest white stock, showing the best taste in its simplicity. Colin was regretful he couldn't say the same for his name, since Quinton insisted it be written in Gaillich also, instead of the way most people pronounced it…Colin William Conor McCoy.

The butler stepped back, allowing Colin to enter. He pushed shut the door. "If you'll wait here, sir, I'll see if His Lordship is receiving."

Colin nodded, watching him disappear down the

hall. He busied himself with looking around, finding nothing of interest. The foyer of Alisdaire Manor was set up much the same as McCoy Hall, larger, of course, more elaborately decorated, but aside from that, it appeared very similar.

Colin ignored his surroundings and concentrated on the hallway where the butler had gone.

In a surprisingly short time, he was back, placing the tray on the nearby table of a breakfront étagère. Colin's card was missing.

"May I take your hat and gloves, sir?" He held out a hand.

Colin doffed his hat, removed his gloves and dropped them inside, handing over both. The butler placed the hat on a nearby hall tree, elaborate with mirrors, coat hooks, and a lift-up seat for storage. He gestured.

"If you'll come this way, please."

Colin fell into step behind him as he led the way down the hall.

Chapter 5

He was led to a set of double sliding doors. The butler knocked, slid open the doors, and stepped inside.

"Mr. Colin McCoy, sir." Stepping back, he waited for Colin to enter.

Feeling very self-conscious, Colin did so. That bothered him a bit. He'd never felt that way before, not when he went with his parents to call on someone, or, at school, whether visiting friends or their parents. As he walked across the threshold, he saw he was now in a library, for the walls were covered with shelves filled with books. He had the absurd feeling he shouldn't be there at all.

Lord Alisdaire was seated behind his desk.

"Sir." He stopped a few feet inside the doors, giving a slight bow. Behind him, he heard the butler draw them closed. "Thank you for receiving me."

"Quite a pleasure…uh…" Lord Alisdaire looked around as if uncertain to whom he was speaking.

"Colin, sir…McCoy," Colin supplied.

His Lordship still held his card. *Why doesn't he simply look at it if he's already forgotten the identity of his caller?*

He wondered why Alisdaire pretended to be so absent-minded, for he was certain the man wasn't as foggy as he appeared. Otherwise, he wouldn't have been entrusted with, and amassed, so much real estate to tend.

Certainly, he hadn't sounded confused when he'd been on the terrace last night.

"That's right," Alisdaire agreed, nodding. He waved the card. "Quinton's boy. The Irish one."

As if Colin's father had an array of sons of different nationalities. Colin was certain he was making reference to Donal's conversion.

"That's right, sir," he agreed, and fell silent again.

"Come in. Sit." Alisdaire gestured to a chair, and Colin gratefully fell into it. "Now, then." His Lordship rose, walked to another, and settled himself. "Did we have business?"

"No, sir, I..." *This is it.* Colin took a deep breath, held it, then let it out slowly while Alisdaire stared at him. "I merely wished to pay my respects, and..." *Get on with it, Col!* a little voice in his mind urged. "...ask your permission to call upon Miss Fiona."

"Fiona?"

Alisdaire's voice went up in seeming shock. Colin wasn't certain if it was that he didn't remember he had a daughter named Fiona or because of who was asking.

"Yes, sir. I was most taken with her at the ball last night, and...and...how is she today? Well over her indisposition, I hope?" he finished.

"She's doing well, probably just a bit of excitement. Her first ball, you know...a little exposure before getting to the big ones in London." Alisdaire brightened a bit. "So, you wish to call on my daughter, eh? With what in mind, exactly?"

Ah, the old man's not as dotty as he seems. Colin wasn't certain whether to be grateful for that or not.

"With the intention of..." Colin sighed and decided to say what he was thinking. "I wish you to know I'm not my brother, sir. I've led a fairly circumspect life, been no better nor worse than any of the others in my class at university. I don't gamble, and don't consider myself a rake by any definition of the word. I assure you anything I feel for Miss Cleary is entirely honorable…"

He was getting so tired of hearing that word. *What if I were to shout, Nay, I'm totally dishonorable. I want t' take your precious daughter an' strip off all her clothin' an' toss her int' me bed an' have such wonderfully wicked ways with her?*

He finished, "I wish to be given permission to walk out with her, Your Lordship…with the idea of…"

"Lord, you do yammer about, don't you?" His Lordship laughed. "Can't just come out and say 'Alisdaire, I want to court your daughter,' can you?"

"Yes sir, I can do that." Heartened, Colin nodded. "Lord Alisdaire, I wish to court Miss Fiona." He waited, aware his heart was attempting to beat a hole in his chest.

"Permission granted." Alisdaire laughed, amused by his sudden cheek. "She's in the garden."

"Oh. No." Colin leaped to his feet, swayed slightly and abruptly sat down again. "Not today. I merely came to seek your permission, perhaps your blessing. I'm not prepared to…"

"Then we'll see you another day." His Lordship rose, tugging on a bell pull near the hearth.

In a moment, the doors slid open and the butler appeared. "Sir?"

"Pour us a bit of wine," Alisdaire ordered. "A lively one. I believe Mr. McCoy here needs a little pick-me-up."

The butler hastened to the liquor cabinet, opened it, and selected a bottle. He returned with two glasses on a tray, offering one to Colin, one to His Lordship. Colin's hand shook as he took his.

Dolt, you're acting as if you're fifteen again and allowed to have your first glass of wine at dinner.

"Drink up, lad." Alisdaire took a sip, then tossed down the rest.

Colin copied his action, remembering how Quinton had told him wine should always be savored a bit. Nevertheless, he felt it was important he drink as the master of Alisdaire Manor did.

Alisdaire returned his glass to the tray the butler held. Colin did the same. He got to his feet. This time, he was steady.

"Thank you, Your Lordship. May I return…say, tomorrow?"

"Quite eager, aren't you?" Without waiting for an answer, Alisdaire said, without looking around, "Hilton, what's on Miss Fiona's social calendar for tomorrow?"

"I believe she's doing charitable work in one of the villages with Her Ladyship, and Mistress McCoy and her daughter-in-law, sir," Hilton replied. "Then in the afternoon, Master Foyle is coming for tea."

Phelan? Colin's heart sank. His old classmate also had his sights set on Fiona? He hadn't seen his former roommate since leaving university, but he remembered Phelan's success with the lasses. *If he's in th' runnin', I definitely have competition.* He told himself he should've realized he wouldn't be the only one taking notice of Fiona Cleary's charms.

"The day after, perhaps?" he suggested, rather weakly.

"Hilton?"

"Miss Fiona did mention she intended to take

flowers to the church."

Church? That jangled Colin so it was a moment before he realized the butler was speaking of a real church and not the London brothel of his younger days. Odd how thoughts of that place kept rising recently.

"…but I believe her afternoon is free."

"Come for tea," Alisdaire instructed.

"Tea," Colin repeated. "In two days. Thank you, sir."

"See Mr. McCoy out, Hilton." Alisdaire settled back into his chair. "Then come back and pour me another glass."

Chapter 6

The ride back to McCoy Hall was such a jumble of emotion and wild thoughts that by the time he reached home, Colin convinced himself he hadn't a chance.

Fiona was going to be swept off her dear little feet by Phelan Foyle and he'd never get to tell her how he felt...how the moment he saw her, he felt some odd connection boring its way into his heart like a worm into an apple, planting something now spreading throughout his body.

Nay, that wasn't a good simile. It made what he was feeling seem a disease, something wicked, when what he wanted with her had nothing wicked about it.

At all.

After all, if Donal could give up visits to the Church for his quiet little Felicity, then surely whatever occurred in their marriage bed was even more sensual than that happening in a harlot's. That meant the visions he had of Fiona in his own weren't lewd or evil, but part of the holy plan making up marriage.

For all his years, Colin abruptly felt desperately ignorant...and suddenly isolated. He wished he dared speak in more depth to Donal but feared his brother would laugh at him. He couldn't talk to Quinton because he didn't want his father aware of how he felt, again fearing ridicule. He was also certain Quinton wouldn't believe his sincerity because of its suddenness, and would accuse him of becoming like Padraig.

Damn it, Padraig, why did you have to leave behind a reputation I have to keep denying I want to live up to?

****

Once inside the Hall, Colin decided to meet things head-on. Whether he was ridiculed or not, he made his way to Quinton's study, knocked on the door, and when his father called, went in.

"Da, I need t' speak with you." Best to dive right in and none of this fiddle-farting around.

"Oh?" Quinton appeared to be in the midst of going over the ledgers for the various farms.

There were at least a dozen of the thick account books on the edge of the desk. Next to them was a stack of letters. Colin glanced at those, seeing one making his heart beat in a different way. It looked like one of the letters from America, like those Padraig sent. They arrived sporadically, usually not more than one a year. Quinton generally relayed from them whatever information he felt the family should know. He'd never denied any of them the right to correspond with Padraig, though as far as Colin knew, only he had sent even one letter to the exile. Quinton had probably written three letters to his absent son in the near ten years he'd been gone.

Quinton closed the ledger and that brought Colin back to the reason for his intrusion into his father's business.

"What can I do for you, lad? Truly, I'll welcome somethin' t' take me mind from these accounts. You know how I dislike doin' th' thin's."

Colin knew that very well. Quinton never liked anything dealing with sums or ciphering. That was why he was so grateful Colin was good with numbers. He'd mentioned several times, and not very subtly, how he'd like his third son to become his clerk. So far, Colin pretended not to hear.

"Father, I'd done somethin' t'day, an' I'm not certain how 'tis going t' turn out. I may have made a great mistake…an' I need your advice."

Quinton stiffened at that. "Does this have to do with Fiona Cleary?"

Lord, how did he come to that conclusion so fast?

"I saw how you were watchin' her all evenin', lad, an' after that *needs some air* ruse…" Quinton got to his feet, sighing heavily. "I suppose I should've expected it. You always idolized Padraig, an' now you're tryin' t' follow in his footsteps."

He came around the desk, leaning against it as if bracing himself for bad news.

"What have you done, an' how much is it goin' t' cost me?"

For the briefest moment, Colin didn't speak, couldn't. That his father would automatically assume he'd committed some act bringing shame to the family angered him. In the next minute, he decided this time, he was going to tell his father exactly how he felt about that.

"Sir, I resent that remark. An' I believe you owe me an apology. How dare you traduce me an' paint me with th' same brush me braithur seems t' glory in wieldin' against himself? I've done naithin' t' bring shame on th' McCoy Dúiche an' I ne'er intend ta. You've judged me afore me trial, and I believe…right now, afore I explain what I *have* done, you should ask me forgiveness for sayin' that."

He stood there, shocked that he'd dare speak to his

father so, and further taken aback by the stunned expression on Quinton's face.

"Well now…" Quinton managed to say. "I'm glad t' hear you've not dishonored th' girl at least. Though I would've wondered when you managed it since you only met yesterday. E'en Padraig ne'er worked *that* fast."

He straightened.

"Very well, Colin." His words came with difficulty. "I offer me amends for what I said. 'Twas unjust o' me t' compare you t' your braithur when you've ne'er given me cause t' do so. Will you accept me apology?"

Colin bit his lip. He was very aware what it cost Quinton to say those words.

"Yes, Da, I will," he answered. "Because I think I understand what it meant when you sent Padraig away an' you don't want t' have t' do that again."

"What is it you have t' tell me?" Quinton actually looked relieved.

"Sit down, Da."

Quinton obeyed, dropping into the nearest chair without questioning that request.

"Sir…" Colin smiled. "I went t' Alisdaire Manor t'day, an' asked permission t' pay court t' Miss Fiona."

Quinton stared at him. He didn't speak.

"Da? Say somethin'."

"What did Alisdaire say?" That question asked so faintly was nothing like his father's usual hearty delivery.

"He didn't say nay." Colin fairly shouted in glee. "I'm t' return on Thursday for tea an' possibly a walk in th' garden."

"Lord, that's movin' fast," Quinton muttered. "I can't believe…"

"His Lordship suggested it," Colin explained.

"Well, that's good then." Quinton stood, went back around his desk and sat down. "It seems His Lordship's more democratic than I expected." He reopened the ledger. "Thanks for lettin' me know, lad. Now, I've work t' do. Be on your way."

He waved a hand, dismissing Colin as if he were eight instead of twenty-eight.

Colin went out, but there was no anger at his father's abrupt dismissal. He hoped he was guessing correctly that Quinton was affected by the fact his youngest son was now contemplating taking one of the most important steps in life. His father was an emotional man, and had always been a loud and laughing one. His argument in that group at the ball before they'd discovered Fiona and Colin's absence was proof of that as well as the many shouts behind closed doors he'd had with Padraig. Sending Padraig away had hurt him immensely. After that, where matters of extreme feelings were concerned, he tended to act as if they were of bare importance.

That was one reason Colin tried to behave. He was doing penance for the unhappiness Padraig left behind.

****

That night at supper, with everyone present and their full plates before them, Quinton got to his feet, tapping a spoon lightly against his wine glass. "I've a few things t' relate."

They all quieted, looking at him expectantly. Before the meal was the time when Quinton would tell them of news from the papers.

As the two other adult males currently in the household, Donal and Colin would already be aware, of course, since they read the papers, also.

After the news was received from the post carrier and ironed by Cormac to smooth out the folds and wrinkles, it was delivered to the master. Once Quinton read each page thoroughly, his sons could peruse them at their leisure.

Màiri and Felicity weren't allowed to read the papers because they contained subject matter considered so violent or blunt in nature as to shock female sensibilities. At the supper table, Quinton delivered a censored version of what he thought his wife and daughter-in-law should know.

This time, however, instead of speaking, he stared at Colin with such intensity, Donal prompted, "What news on the home front, sir? Anything interesting happening in London?"

He and Felicity had been away from there for over a week now.

"Not much in London," Quinton muttered. "But something definitely a li'l closer t' home."

"What, exactly?" Màiri spoke up.

"Well…our Colin has decided t' take matrimonial steps."

Everyone turned to stare at Colin who felt himself flush.

"Oh?" Donal prompted.

"As o' this comin' Thursday, he's going t' be callin' on Fiona Cleary."

"Oh, Colin!" His mother was out of her chair, not waiting for the footman to assist her. She hurried around the table, seizing her son as he also stood, hugging him tightly. "This makes me so happy."

"Thank you, Mama." Colin managed a whisper.

As she returned to her seat, he cautioned, "Don't

start countin' grandchildren just yet, though," trying to inject a light note because he feared his mother might start crying in her happiness. Màiri-Caitlin McCoy was prone to do that, much to her children's embarrassment, as well as her husband's.

"Miss Fiona may decide she doesn't want me. She does have ithir suitors."

"Not if she has any sense," Màiri retorted.

Chapter 7

"Lemon or milk, Mr. McCoy?" Lady Alisdaire looked expectantly at Colin.

"Neither." He didn't hesitate, saying the little speech he'd planned on the way over, something culled from a long-ago conversation with Donal. "I prefer not to adulterate the true taste of the brew."

"Ah, a purist." Alisdaire looked approving. "Not too many of those in these parts. Seems everyone wants to add something…lemon, sugar, milk…even cinnamon."

From the sharp glance Fiona gave her father, Colin surmised she was one of those guilty of using that last ingredient.

"My brother prefers his tea plain." Colin accepted the cup from Her Ladyship, nodding his thanks, as he modulated his accent into one a bit more refined. "He initiated me into the proper way to drink it during one of his trips home from school."

Not too much of a lie. Donal had told him that fact, but Colin laughed at him and added two spoonfuls of sugar in defiance.

"School…yes," Alisdaire muttered. "You went away for instruction also, didn't you, McCoy?" He seemingly continued to have trouble remembering Colin's given name so had reverted to simply calling him by his family one.

"Yes, sir. I matriculated at Cambridge as Donal

did." The inference being, of course, not going elsewhere as Padraig had.

"What did you read?" Her Ladyship asked.

"Mathematics, ma'am." Colin tried not to show his surprise that she would be interested in what he had studied.

As she exchanged a glance with Alisdaire, he decided they had divided between them the interrogation he, as their daughter's would-be suitor, was to be given.

"Mathematics? Oh."

Her hands fluttered slightly, a vague female gesture he'd seen her make at the ball. Colin had a good idea Lady Alisdaire was no more flighty than her husband was absent-minded.

"Numbers…that would distress me so. I fear I've no head for sums. Keeping the household accounts, that's enough for my poor mind."

"That's a pity." Colin pitched his voice to hold sympathy and not the usual condescension a man might use in regard to a female's admitted weakness. "Numbers can be fascinating once one comes to understand them. I find them so." He glanced at Fiona who appeared about to speak and hoped he was interpreting her expression correctly. "Don't you think so, Miss Fiona?"

"I most certainly do." She snapped eagerly, as if she'd been waiting for him to ask. "Someone once called arithmetic 'the romance of numbers' and though I wouldn't say I understand higher mathematics such as algebra, trigonometry and such, I do find doing sums and simple ciphering enjoyable."

She glanced at Alisdaire and there was something challenging in her gaze.

"In fact, I might dare say it's soothing."

Lady Alisdaire offered the cake plate. Colin declined with a shake of his head.

"That's an interesting observation." Colin looked at her with an expression bordering on astonishment, then struggled to conceal it but saw by her slight smile he'd failed. "I once thou…"

"What do you plan to do with your degree?" Alisdaire interrupted. He was frowning now.

Colin had a sudden insight His Lordship didn't wish Fiona to reveal she had enough brain-power to actually like math, for fear it would discourage young men from courting her. After all, no one wanted a wife who might be as smart as he, or perhaps more so, and the ability to understand numbers definitely hinted at that. After all, where would a woman ever use such a thing? It definitely wouldn't help her in childbearing, which would be her main function in her husband's life, tending his house and home being second.

"Hadn't really given it much thought…" Colin began. As Alisdaire's frown transformed into a scowl, he continued, smoothly, "…until recently."

That made his Lordship perk up slightly.

"My father's in dire need of an accounting clerk, and…" Here he laughed a little self-deprecatingly. "…I've been considering telling him I'd be glad to help out, providing he doesn't treat me like one of the hired help, of course."

Alisdaire joined in his laughter. Colin realized he hadn't tasted his tea, after his grand words concerning it, and raised the delicate cup, sipping at what he considered a tasteless beverage. He wondered how it would be with a pinch of cinnamon added.

Lowering the cup, he glanced around, looking past Fiona and her mother to the garden and the flower-encased walls behind them.

"You've some lovely flowers, Your Ladyship. Do I detect…" He raised his head, sniffing delicately. "…roses?" he nodded. "Yes, quite a variety, I believe, if those luscious fragrances are any indication."

"Oh, yes." As he expected, Her Ladyship preened slightly at mention of the roses of which she was inordinately proud. "I have over fifteen varieties."

"Would it be forward of me to ask if I might see them?" He gave her an earnest look, the one always convincing his father's cook he desperately needed that cookie he'd been forbidden by his mother. "My mother has roses, also, as I'm certain you're aware, but I'm sure she hasn't any as lovely as yours."

"As a matter of fact, I have three new varieties, some cuttings of which Robert recently had brought from our townhouse in London. I believe Màiri hasn't seen those yet. She didn't even have time for tea yesterday because we got back from our charity work so late." Lady Alisdaire's attitude hinted it would be a *coup* on her part for Màiri's son to tell his mother he'd seen the new roses first. She half-rose. "If you'd care to come this way…"

Colin also rose, not betraying by a grimace how he'd hoped Fiona would be the one giving him the garden tour. Out of the corner of his eye, he saw Alisdaire gesture.

"…or perhaps Fiona could show you?" She sat down again. "I daresay this afternoon sun seems a bit too hot for me."

Though apparently not too warm for her daughter, the unspoken words hinted.

"Thank you." Colin bowed. "I'd be most appreciative."

He glanced at Fiona, who rose gracefully. Colin skirted the table, going around Alisdaire and Her Ladyship and coming to Fiona's side. Bowing again, he held out his arm.

"Miss Cleary, would you grace me by being my guide through your mother's rose garden?"

"Certainly, Mr. McCoy."

Gently she placed her hand on his arm. He managed to stifle the delicious shudder his skin wanted to give at her touch, even through the layers of jacket sleeve and shirt.

He stepped back so she could take her place beside him.

"I'll make certain we stay in sight at all times," he promised Alisdaire while mentally planning to get out of their line of vision as soon as humanly possible.

"This way, Mr. McCoy." Fiona inclined her head toward the path leading from the little courtyard into the garden.

****

They'd gone only a few feet before he asked, "Do you really like mathematics?"

"Oh, yes," she answered. "Though I doubt I'm anywhere in your league." She laughed. "No one's going to be awarding me a degree, I don't imagine." Her eyes twinkled. "I especially like algebra."

"Where would you learn algebra?" He didn't mean to sound so astonished, but it was unusual for a young lady to be taught that subject. Indeed, most he knew were coached along the lines of deportment and etiquettes, as well as keeping household expenses, noting how much foodstuffs cost, and things of that nature.

"My brother's tutor," she explained. "I used to come into the schoolroom and sit in a corner and listen to him instruct Samuel. Afterward, he'd often answer any questions I had and occasionally let me work a problem or two."

Colin thought about that. He could envision a little moppet in a pink muslin gown and pinafore, earnestly wielding a quill, the tip of her tongue caught between her teeth as she tackled a problem that might've given her brother trouble...and solving it, much to his chagrin.

"Did you really want to see Mamma's flowers?" Her question brought him out of his reverie.

He decided to tell the truth. "Not really, but 'twas th' quickest an' easiest way t' get you more or less alone, though for a moment there I thought I'd outsmarted meself."

"Then I suppose you didn't see Father..."

"Yes, I did. An' I thank His Lordship for bein' so generous on me first visit."

"He's not being generous. He considers himself being helpful. I think he likes you."

"That's good, considerin' he can't seem t' remember me name."

"He does that to everyone," she countered. "He says that's the best way to keep someone off-guard. Mr. McCoy, what's happened to your accent?

Oh, damn. He'd been so comfortable in her company, he'd briefly forgotten to use that *received pronunciation* he'd learned at school. *Well, nothin' for it but t' tell th' truth.*

"I suppressed it," he confessed. "Didn't want your faithur thinkin' I sounded like some bogtrotter. But 'tis comin' back now. Can't stay repressed for long, it appears." He smiled. "Or perhaps 'tis your lovely presence settin' it free."

"Frankly, I much prefer hearing it than that rather supercilious way you were speaking before."

"Here now, an' I thought I sounded so elegant."

"Oh, you did. But it isn't *you*..." She gave him a direct stare sending a silent shiver through him. "And I much prefer you."

"An' what exactly is *me*?"

"Someone who doesn't put on airs, who speaks plainly in his own beautiful voice, and doesn't pretend to be what he isn't."

"You think me voice is beautiful?" *Here now, I'm supposed to be givin' th' compliments*, his mind protested.

"Didn't I just say so?"

They continued down the path as she spoke, his longer legs adjusting their strides to match her slower ones.

"Though I suppose playing a bit of a masquerade is called for when you're trying to impress someone. You *are* trying to impress Father, aren't you?"

"Lass, you can't imagine how I'm tryin' t' impress him." He stopped, glancing back. Both His Lordship and Lady Alisdaire were watching them. *Damn it.* He took a deep breath. "I'm glad there aren't many flowers in this part o' th' garden."

They were surrounded by bordered plants and greenery but no blossoms, thank goodness.

"Why?"

"Because the scent o' all o' them was drownin' out your own beautiful smell...I mean..." He floundered slightly, thinking that sounded more like an insult than a compliment, and recovered. "What is that fragrance, anyway?"

"It's lavender." She obviously found his stuttering amusing.

"Really? Me maithur uses that, but on you..." He inhaled again and closed his eyes, as if transported elsewhere. "...it smells much, much better."

"I've practically grown up with it," she explained, not fluttering and thanking him as some other girl might. "When I was a baby, I was so cranky my nurse used to bathe me in lavender water to help me sleep..."

"You? Cranky?" He pretended disbelief. "Ne'er."

She tapped his arm lightly in reprimand. He dared grin guiltily.

"When I got older, it only seemed natural to ask my father to buy me a flacon for my birthday. I've been using it ever since."

"An' from now on, e'ery time I get th' briefest whiff o' lavender, no matter who's wearin' it, I'll think o' you."

"Oh, you're such a flatterer. Have you ever been to Blarney Castle?"

"I'm afraid not. I guess I come by any glibness I have by natural means." He thought of Padraig and how he truly had "the gift of gab," as if he'd been blest with knowing just what to say and when to say it.

Glancing back, he saw a servant come from inside the house, bowing and speaking to Alisdaire. His Lordship rose, said something to his wife, and went inside. The moment the door closed, Lady Alisdaire turned her attention from the two in the garden to the remainder of the uneaten cakes on the tray before her.

She selected one and bit into it.

At last.

There was a sudden twist to the garden path. The wall followed the same way. They walked three feet more and abruptly were out of sight of Her Ladyship and the table.

"What's over there?" Colin turned his attention outside the wall.

He could see plainly there was a small cleared space of land and then the beginnings of a wood, overgrown with slender trees close together, high green bracken, and dangling vines.

"I think you can see," she answered.

They stopped.

Colin leaned against the wall, peering over it. "Seems a fair place for youngsters to play...hide and seek, blind man's buff..."

"It's a great place to play," she agreed. "There's a little brook running through the wood. When I was small, my brother and I would slip away and go there. I'd remove my stockings and wade in the water while Samuel tried to capture minnows."

"Was the water cold?"

"Very." She exaggerated a quaver. "Like liquid ice." She shivered again.

To prevent the abruptly arousing image of a grown-up Fiona, stockings in hand, bare legs gleaming as she walked with raised skirts through running water, Colin asked, "Did Samuel catch many? Minnows, I mean?"

"Not usually, and those he did I always made him release back into the water." She sighed. "I haven't been back there in many years. It was such fun. Sometimes becoming an adult is tedious because it prevents one from doing enjoyable things."

"I agree." He leaned toward her slightly, lowering his voice. "Would you like t' go again? Now?"

It wasn't a high wall, coming only to his waist. He could get over it easily, but someone in an afternoon tea gown…

"You mean…" She glanced back, realized they were out of sight of the house, and stopped.

"I do." Putting both hands on the wall, Colin pulled himself onto it. He sat there a moment, then threw his legs over and slid to the ground, landing in a gathering of fern fronds and goldenrod. He held out his hands. "Come on, lass. Let's be children again for a bit."

Surprisingly, she didn't protest, simply glanced back again, then reached for his hands. He caught her about the waist and lifted her over, seeing her astonishment as he seemed to do it so easily. It wasn't difficult. She was as light as a child.

She gave a delighted laugh as he swung her from wall to ground, then immediately stifled the sound. Colin spun her around, enjoying the feel of his hands on her waist, not wishing to let her go.

"You realize we shouldn't be doing this," she said in a loud whisper. "If Father finds out…"

"Then we'll have t' be careful that he doesn't, won't we?" He set her down.

They stood looking at each other, smiling conspirators, two youngsters having put something over on the adults.

"Now then, where's this brook?"

Taking his hand, she led him into the wood.

Chapter 8

It would've been so easy for a seduction, Colin realized.

The wood was shadowed but not dark, sunlight filtering through the trees making flickering dapples on their arms and faces. Except for the occasional rustling of something scurrying through the leaves underfoot, or the flutter of a bird's wing accompanied by a chirp or two, it was very quiet. The ferns were thick and tall, some nearly three feet high, curling and leafy, giving the aspect of how he imagined a jungle looked. It was definitely a fantasy-tinged place…where one might expect to come upon one of the faery folk fluttering by on a butterfly's back, or a leprechaun lugging home his pot o' gold.

It would've been an ideal spot to whisper sweet nothings into a lass's ear and convince her he was dying for her love, and soon have her beneath him on the moss while he had his way, all the while gasping promises he didn't mean into her ear.

That's what Padraig would've done, but…

Colin surprised himself by admitting he didn't want that. That is, he wanted it but he wasn't going to be foolish enough to attempt it, because all he truly wished in that moment was to be alone with Fiona and away from her parents' watchful eyes…where they could talk without him using that false voice and she could say the things actually on her mind, and not merely what her father wished her to say. He didn't imagine she'd ever told any other young man, certainly not Phelan, that she liked mathematics. That little glance at Alisdaire had spoken volumes.

To get his mind off bodies rolling in the grass, he launched a conversation about some subject. He never later remembered what, except that it was far, far away from love, lust, and seduction, or anything along those lines. The things they did talk about weren't so world-shattering, anyway, simply…safe.

There was a fallen tree near the brook. He dusted it with his handkerchief to rid it of any loose bark or insects. She seated herself, settling her skirts, and he sat beside her and they talked. Sometime during the conversation, he told her how Quinton wished him to become his clerk, and how he'd never thought of doing such a thing until that day.

"I wouldn't consider it demeanin' t' help me faithur, though I definitely wouldn't want t' be employed as a clerk o' any kind by anyone else," he said, vehemently. "Would you look down on me if I told e'eryone I'm a clerk, Miss Cleary?"

"No, Mr. McCoy, I wouldn't," she answered, and he felt she meant it. "I have a feeling no matter what you do, it would never be demeaning, even if you were a street sweeper."

"Ah now…let's hope I ne'er have t' do that." He raised his eyes heavenward and put his hands together prayerfully.

She laughed at that, as if envisioning him with dust on his face and his hands grimy from wielding a broom as he dashed in front of pedestrians and cleared the way of mud, debris, and whatever else for a penny or two.

"Fiona, may I speak seriously?"

"I thought we were, Colin." Somewhere, they'd dispensed with titles and were talking more familiarly.

"Aye, I suppose we were, but I mean, truly seriously."

"Certainly." She frowned, more from his change in manner than at his words.

"Th' moment I saw you at the ball...I swear I ne'er felt like that afore, an' it shocked me. I thought you were...you looked so... When you spoke, chidin' your faithur for not completin' his introduction..." He stopped. "I'm sayin' this all wrong."

She didn't answer.

He tried again. "I know you're aware o' me braithur Padraig's reputation, if not all th' devilment he did..."

"Only vaguely," she admitted. "I suppose Father thought the extent of your brother's...uh...depredations..." Her mouth quirked slightly as if she were uncertain that was the proper word to use. "...were too lurid for my ears. Samuel told me a bit but even his version was greatly censored, I imagine. Did he really climb down an ivy vine to escape from Lady Cornwell's bedchamber? With his breeches tied around his neck?"

"Lord, if Samuel told you that, he ought t' be beat!" Colin exclaimed. "He calls that *censorship*?"

"He recounted it with the most envy," she said, lips trembling.

Colin wondered if that tremor was from disapproval or amusement.

"I'm afraid he did," he admitted, then hurried on, "I don't want t' talk about Padraig, except t' assure you I'm naithin' like him. I…"

He got up, walking to the brook's edge. It burbled and gurgled on its way, unmindful of the young man standing on its banks, about to make the most important declaration of his life up to that point.

"I'm no saint, Fiona…though I'm not th' worse sinner, aithur, I hope. 'Tis like I told your faithur, I suppose I'm no worse nor any better than any young man me age, but…" Shaking his head, he looked back at her. "That kiss I gave you at th' ball, 'twas a pledge, you know."

"What kind of pledge?"

He thought he saw hope flicker in her eyes.

"That I truly have proper an' respectful feelin's for you, an' I'll ne'er do anythin' t' cause a question t' arise about your honor…"

"…and yet you brought me *here*. To this very secluded spot." She gestured around them. "Out of sight of our chaperones."

"Aye, I did," he agreed.

"To do what, exactly?" She looked up at him, meeting his gaze steadfastly. "Since you're being so candid, Mr. McCoy. Tell me the truth. Why did you bring me here?"

"To tell you I love you, lass." Colin stopped, mouth falling open. *What did I just say? Oh God!*

"You…love me?" She sounded as if she couldn't believe it, either.

"…an' that's why I'm now goin' t' take you back."

He seized her hand, pulling her to her feet, speaking rapidly as he tried to dispel the awful sickening rush coiling through his belly, trying to hide the fear galloping in, and get his mind back to working properly. At the moment, it felt stunned, as if he'd been struck betwixt the eyes by an iron-solid fist.

Lord, why did I say that?

"...afore those chaperones, specifically your faithur, discover we're gone an' think th' worse."

At a fast clip, those long legs carried him back the way they came, toward the wall, while he asked himself, *What am I running from?* Or was he running *toward* something?

Briefly, Colin felt like a riderless horse, bit between his teeth, galloping blindly with no one to stop his headlong, and perhaps destructive, charge.

"Please, slow down," she protested, her voice breaking through his panic. "Else I may trip and ruin a stocking, and how will I explain that?"

That commonplace question soothed him and brought back sanity. He slowed his pace. The wall came into sight. Colin put his hands around Fiona's waist, speaking rapidly and with frightening sincerity.

"I want t' court you, Fiona. Woo an' win you...away from Phelan Foyle or anyone else who's waitin in line."

"Colin, you don't have to worry about Phelan Foyle," she assured him, placing a hand on his arm as his own tightened about her waist. "You won out over him the moment you took the first step of that waltz."

"Oh, lass."

He bent and kissed her, a kiss much like the quick and furtive one he'd given her at the ball, then hoisted her over the wall and to the other side. Colin followed, caught her again and kissed her a bit more thoroughly this time, looking pleased as he released her and she stepped back, taking a deep breath.

A door slammed. Lord Alisdaire's voice floated to

them. Colin caught Fiona's hand and stepped onto the path so they were in sight as he heard His Lordship's footsteps on the flagstones. He looked around frantically for a subject, gaze falling on a small bushy plant sporting yellow daisy-like flowers.

"What's this one called?" he asked. There were nearly three dozen of them lining the border at the base of the wall.

"That's a marguerite," she answered, understanding what he was attempting.

Colin knelt and snapped off one as Alisdaire appeared at the curve of the wall.

"Fiona…" He stopped as he saw Colin on his knees before his daughter, offering her the little yellow flower. "Here now. Not proposing already, are you?"

"Uh…no, sir…" Colin got to his feet, dusting his knees. "Miss Fiona was explainin' to me about marguerites an' I gave in t' th' temptation t' pick one for her." He looked suitably anxious. "I trust that was all right? Her Ladyship won't mind?"

"Indeed not," Alisdaire assured him. "Both Fiona and my wife pick flowers every day to decorate the house." He reached for Fiona's arm, placing it securely on his. "I do think it's time you young people returned to the courtyard, however. Her Ladyship was beginning to worry when she couldn't see you, though she knows the path winds a bit here."

He started back the way he'd come. Colin followed, carefully not looking at Fiona.

"By the way," His Lordship continued. "What happened to your voice?"

"I convinced Mr. McCoy he should sound like himself and not like an Englishman, since he isn't one,"

Fiona declared.

"Eh? Well, that's quite right." Alisdaire nodded. "We don't like masquerades in this house." He didn't seem to think his own accent might be suspect. He glanced back at Colin. "Didn't sound as good on you as it does on your brother, anyway."

Back at the tea table, Lady Alisdaire was finishing the last cake as they arrived. "There you are." She brushed crumbs from her lower lip with a delicate tea napkin. "Where were you two? That dratted wall cut you off from my sight."

"We were just on the other side, Mamma," Fiona answered. "Looking at the flowers." She held out the marguerite. "Colin picked this for me."

"I hope you don't mind," Colin put in, in spite of what Alisdaire had said.

"Not at all," Her Ladyship replied. "I believe I'll cut a few to take in." She glanced down. "My dear, what's this?"

"What's what, Mamma?" Fiona's eyes followed her mother's own, as did Alisdaire's.

Colin's heart sank. A few inches of the hem of Fiona's gown hung loose and muddy, the pink muslin discolored, threads unraveling. Alisdaire didn't speak but glanced eloquently at Colin.

"Oh, that." Fiona's tone brushed it aside. "I suppose I did that as we went past that Aurora rose. It has the thickest thorns, and my skirt got caught on one. As for the mud…" She shrugged. "The gardeners watered a little too generously this morning, I'm afraid."

"That's right," Colin took up the tale. "I remember, you tugged at it and it came free." He looked apologetic. "I didn't realize it had torn…" He glanced at his own knees. "I'm surprised I didn't muddy my trousers when I knelt to pick that blossom."

He decided he'd better shut up before he said too much.

"You're right, Fiona. That particular plant does have the most horrendous thorns, almost like needles." Her Ladyship sighed. "I suppose I'll have to ask one of the gardeners to remove most of them." She got to her feet. "Yes, I'll have him do it tomorrow. First thing. As for the mud…we have to water the flowers. Anyway, the gown will wash."

Fiona exchanged a glance with Colin, smiling as he let out a slow sigh, realizing only then he'd been holding his breath. Lord Alisdaire glanced at him. He took that as his cue to leave.

"Your Ladyship, Lord Alisdaire, Miss Fiona…" He bowed over Her Ladyship's hand, kissed Fiona's, then nodded to His Lordship. "I thank you for allowin' me t' call t'day." He gave Alisdaire a beseeching and earnest stare. "Might I dare ask if I have permission t' call again? Say, this comin' Saturday, an' take Miss Fiona for a drive?"

"Rushing things a bit, ain't you, boy?" Alisdaire asked, bluntly.

"Perhaps it seems so t' you, sir, but t' me…" The shake of Colin's head bespoke confusion. "Truly, sir…an' I know Miss Fiona will probably think me daft, but th' mere thought o' how far away Saturday is makes it seem eons."

"I assure you, I think no such thing, Mr. McCoy. Anyway, Saturday is only two days away, not a thousand years." Fiona leaned against her father's arm, clasping it tightly. He apparently liked that, for he smiled and placed his hand over hers.

"The carriage is large enough for her abigail t' go along, too," Colin added. "I wouldn't think o' havin' her ride with me unchaperoned."

"Certainly not," Alisdaire agreed.

Colin wondered if that was a twinkle in His Lordship's eyes, or merely the sunlight glittering in them.

"Saturday morning, around nine, Mr. McCoy. Perhaps a short drive down one of the scenic lanes between here and your father's estate…that picnic area. Yes, that's perfect. There are certain to be people there, so you two won't be alone if you decide to get out and walk."

"Yes sir…picnic area…scenic lane… Thank you, Your Lordship."

Colin turned, saw Hilton standing in the doorway, and allowed the butler to lead him to the front door where a groom waited, having brought his horse around.

Behind him, he heard Lady Alisdaire ask, "Whatever happened to his accent?"

He rode back to McCoy Hall with a heart so light he was glad he was holding the reins. Otherwise he might've floated away.

The first person he met upon arriving home was Donal.

"My God, you look gobsmacked," his brother exclaimed.

"Thank you," Colin replied with dignity. "You're no beauty yourself."

"Colin, I mean it. You've the look of a man who's just been kicked by a horse. In a most personal place."

"I have…" He got no further.

"Come into the parlor." Donal grabbed his arm. "Sit down. I'll have Cormac send someone for the doctor. Are you bleeding anywhere?"

He dragged Colin to the parlor as he spoke.

"How can you even walk?" He looked around, didn't see the butler, and bellowed, "Cormac!"

"Donal…Donal!" Colin laughed. He'd never seen his brother this emotional. Not even when he witnessed Colin fall off his horse while he was being taught to jump.

His brother stopped, staring at him. "Oh, God, you're hysterical."

He raised a hand, preparing to administering a sanity-restoring slap.

"Nay, I'm…" He caught Donal's hand, pulling it down. "I'm only in love, I'm afraid, an' I truly ne'er thought 'twould hurt so good. God, Donal, how will I survive until th' proper time passes so I can speak to His Lordship?"

"Love?" Donal reacted by throwing off his grasp. "That's all this is?" He backed away. "And here I thought you were dying. That you'd been…"

His expression went from concerned to furious.

"Unless you made a complete fool of yourself today, I suppose any time after a month would be a long enough wait before you fully commit yourself. Why ask me?" That was delivered with angry asperity. "Speak to Father. It concerns him more, anyway."

He straightened his jacket and brushed back his hair, which had fallen onto his forehead as he hustled Colin into the parlor. Spinning on his heel, back so stiff it appeared he had a board sewn into his coat, he stalked out, leaving Colin sitting there.

Chapter 9

Taking her hand, Colin assisted Fiona's abigail into the curricle.

Edith was a little thing, probably not more than fifteen years of age. She reminded him of a wild bunny, all big eyes and soft brown hair wrapped in a gray bonnet and gown. She clutched her shawl tightly about her and looked around with an expression that could've been either awe because this was her first ride in such a sporting vehicle or fear at the weightiness of the task of being a chaperone.

Fiona had protested briefly because she feared there wasn't room in the curricle for three persons.

"Of course, there is," Colin assured her.

He studied the dress she was wearing, thinking he might've spoken too soon. Fiona was clad in a demure little rose-pink day dress he thought made her fair complexion even fairer but the sheer *volume* of it was overwhelming.

The dress itself was rather plain and undecorated, though its pagoda sleeves with ruffled lace *engageantes* from elbow to wrist and high lace-embellished collar made up for that. Over it all, she wore a short-sleeved jacket. The skirt of the dress was full, however. Briefly, he feared between her and Edith and the width of their skirts, though Edith's were by no means as full as Fiona's, there might be no room in the little carriage for *him.*

"Edith here is too small t' be considered an adult." He decided to bluff his way through this minor problem before someone else noticed. "She won't take up much room." He was also thinking that with three people crowded onto the seat, Fiona would have to sit closer to him to give the maid breathing room.

Making certain the girl was settled, he turned to Fiona, again offering his hand. She smiled and placed her own in his, allowing him to steady her as she climbed into the curricle.

"I must say you look most handsome today, Mr. McCoy." Lady Alisdaire accompanied them onto the front stoop, along with her son, Samuel, who'd arrived home the day before.

"Thank you, ma'am." Colin nodded an appreciative bow.

"You're right, Mamma. That's certainly a fine-looking ditto suit," Samuel put in. He caught the lapel of his dark brown morning coat with its cutaway front. "Almost as sharp as mine."

"Good o' you t' say that, Samuel." Colin was well aware his own clothing, from his gray felt top hat and black cutaway to his gray waistcoat and trousers, was the latest style. He also knew Samuel was guying him a bit. "Since we have th' same tailors both here an' in London."

They laughed easily together, two young men who, while not close chums, were comfortable in each other's company because of their relationship to Fiona, and also having various mutual acquaintances at Cambridge.

"You're certain this vehicle is safe, Mr. McCoy?" Behind her son, Lady Alisdaire was putting in her two pennies-worth of motherly concern. "I've heard curricles are notorious for capsizing."

"You're thinking of sailboats, Mamma," Samuel put in. "The worst thing a curricle can do is overturn."

"Oh! Well, I don't want it to do that, either," Her Ladyship worried. "Fiona, perhaps you shouldn't go."

Thank you, Samuel. Colin shot a dagger-filled glance at Fiona's brother. The last thing he wanted was to be confined to Alisdaire Manor's stuffy parlor when such a beautiful day presented itself.

Samuel merely shrugged as if to say, *Sorry, I thought I was helping.* They both knew the little sports carriages had a notorious reputation for accidents but more from the recklessness of their drivers than some flaw in the design. Samuel, as well as Colin, had been involved in races and each suffered minor mishaps they'd kept from their parents.

Lady Alisdaire placed a hand on the chariot's steps. "Come back inside, my dear. Mr. McCoy may do his visiting in the parlor."

"But Mamma," Fiona protested, turning so she faced her mother and accidentally pushed poor Edith into the corner of the seat.

The little maid huddled as close to the side of the curricle as possible, taking a deep breath as if she had no room for air.

"It's such a beautiful day, and Mr. McCoy promised to take me to see the lake, and…"

"I agree the day is lovely, but if this thing is unsafe…" Her mother rolled her eyes and focused on Colin, taking a deep breath.

"Oh, come, Mamma." Before she could finish, Samuel attempted to make up for possibly spoiling

Colin's plans. "I drive a curricle, also, and you know Papa wouldn't allow that if he thought there was any danger."

Over her head, he looked at Colin as he spoke. Colin nodded approval of his statement.

"Yes, that's true," Her Ladyship agreed. She looked back at Colin. "Very well, Mr. McCoy, you have my permission to continue with your outing, but…" She placed a gentle hand on the one resting against the curricle's wheel. "…do be careful."

"Ma'am, I shall take th' utmost care. Miss Fiona is as precious t' me as she is t' you," Colin assured her. *Perhaps more so.*

Behind his mother, Samuel clasped his hands to his heart and rolled his eyes heavenward. Colin shot him another scowl.

"Be certain I'll drive as carefully as possible."

With that, he climbed into the little carriage, gathered the reins and nodded to the groom who was standing at the head of one of the perfectly matched black-bay hackneys. The groom released the horse's head and stepped back and Colin drove the curricle out of the front courtyard as fast as he could without whipping the horses into a full gallop.

He'd been right. As small as Edith was, it *was* crowded with three, and Fiona leaned against him, entwining her arm with his. That made guiding the horses a bit dicey, but the pair were such veterans to the single axle vehicle that he was certain they could pull it with no help from him whatsoever if it became necessary.

"Is it really dangerous?" Fiona asked as she waved over her shoulder at her mother, then settled into the seat beside him.

"Not in th' least," he lied.

He didn't remove Fiona's arm from his.

****

They hadn't gone far before Fiona put up one hand, as if to shade her eyes from the sun.

"Is it too bright?" Colin asked. "I notice you didn't bring a parasol."

"Oh, Miss," Edith worried. "I knew you should've. Didn't I tell you?"

"Hush, Edith," Fiona interrupted. "No, Mr. McCoy, the sun isn't too bright...yet. If it does become uncomfortable, I'm certain you can put up the top."

"Oooh, Miss, that would be scandalous," Edith protested. "Riding along shut off from view. Her Ladyship certainly wouldn't want to hear that."

"She won't, unless someone tells her...and she'd better not," Fiona snapped. "What could happen? Anyway, that's exactly why you're here, so do be quiet and let's enjoy the drive."

"Yes, Miss." Suitably chastened, Edith crouched in her corner and bit her lip, turning her attention to the scenery rapidly speeding by.

"Wasn't that a bit harsh?" Colin asked, in an undertone.

"Was it?" Fiona didn't appear concerned with how she'd treated the maid. "I don't think so. I've always wanted to ride in a curricle, ever since Samuel described racing his. I imagine I shall want to do it again, and I won't appreciate it if Edith says something to prevent that."

"Why, Miss Fiona." Colin took his attention from the road long enough to give her a glance of mock surprise. "I do believe you're a bit spoiled."

"No, I'm not," Fiona corrected. "I'm greatly spoiled."

They both laughed. Colin flicked the whip, making it snap over the horses' backs though it touched neither's deep red flanks. The pair quickened their paces. Fiona snuggled closer, tightening her grasp on his arm. After a few moments, she dared lean her head against his shoulder.

She was wearing a little pancake of a hat, decorated with tiny bouquets of flowers and satin ribbon streamers that fluttered gaily in the breeze stirred as the horses trotted along. One floated upward, brushing against Colin's earlobe, tickling it.

From Edith's corner came a quick inhalation of breath but the little maid didn't say a word about Fiona's action. *Good girl,* Colin thought, enjoying Fiona's closeness so much he also might've spoken harshly to the maid if she'd dare object.

They'd traveled a bit before Fiona spoke again.

"You handle the horses quite easily."

"Me faithur taught me when I was young."

"I've often ridden with Samuel. He's a good driver, also."

Colin was tempted to ask if they were speaking of the same Samuel, the young man who'd raced around the fountain in the town square of Little Epping and ended up being dumped into the water when he tried to turn the horses too sharply and the curricle tipped over. He didn't comment.

"I've often wished I knew how to handle horses."

"Would you like t' learn how t' drive, Miss Fiona?" Colin held out the reins.

"You'll teach me?" In her eagerness, she nearly pulled them from his hand.

From Edith's corner, there was another slight gasp. Colin decided the abigail was a passive disapprover, more apt to make sounds of reprimand than actually speaking them.

"Easy," he cautioned, carefully regaining the reins and placing the lines in her left hand.

"I don't use both?" she asked.

He shook his head. "These are made for a man's hands so they're a bit wide for you t' hold, but I think we can manage. Hold the reins like this."

He demonstrated by placing his left hand so his elbow and his curled fingers rested against his waistcoat front.

"With th' lines just so." He placed one in her hand, at her thumb and forefinger. "This is th' lead rein, an' this…" He inserted the other between her fore and third fingers. "…is th' wheel rein."

She clasped them tightly.

"You don't need t' grasp them as if th' horses are going t' jerk them from your hand," he cautioned.

Her grip relaxed.

"Simply hold firmly, in case something untoward happens, an' so th' horses are aware you're in command."

With that, he put his hand over hers, turning it slightly, giving the horses the office. They veered a bit to the right, coming closer to the edge of the road. Colin quickly turned her hand and the horses moved back to their original place without stopping.

"See?"

"Oh, that's so wonderful." She moved closer.

Through the voluminous skirt, her knee jostled his. Colin stifled a faint groan of pleasure.

"Do I need the whip?"

"Do you think you do?"

"I notice you put it back into its holder." She nodded around him to the little depression in the curricle's side where the whip was firmly fastened.

"I try not t' use a whip very much unless I'm racin'."

"Samuel always uses one."

"That's where your brother an' I differ in our opinions on drivin'." Colin didn't add that Samuel raced so often, he automatically caught up the whip the moment he got into his curricle. He released Fiona's hand. "Now then, let's see you handle th' team the rest o' th' way t' th' lake."

She glanced at the horses and back at him.

"Don't worry. I'll be here if you need assistance."

There was a slight snort from Edith as if to say, *Where else would you be unless you plan on jumping onto the road?*

Colin shot the maid a wink and she blushed.

The turn-off to the lake appeared. With Colin calling out instructions, Fiona guided the horses around the curve, laughing delightedly as the animals obeyed without the slightest hesitation.

The lake, fed by the River Arra running through Tipperary, came into sight...wide, blue, and surrounded by activity even this early in the morning.

Chapter 10

"I think I'd best take back th' reins." Colin slid them out of Fiona's hand.

Reluctantly, she released them, making a little grimace of disappointment.

"In case there's someone around who might consider it unseemly for a young lady t' be handlin' horses," he explained.

Edith's sigh approved his decision.

Down the hill and away from the road, there was a small dock with rowboats tied to it. Two boats were on the lake. One held a young man energetically pulling on the oars while his sweetheart sat in the bow on a cushion, trailing her fingers in the water. The other held two couples. The young ladies, carefully protected by their parasols, were calling out and waving to friends on shore. Their companions sat at the stern of the boat, both manning the oars in skillful coordination, sending it fairly skimming over the surface.

Near the bank, several picnic blankets had been spread, baskets opened and their contents displayed. Couples sat, nibbling on sandwiches and sipping from picnic carafes. One or two of the more adventurous young men, clad in bathing costumes consisting of short-sleeved shirts and knee-length flannel breeches sporting bright stripes, were wading into the water. A particularly bold lad swam a few feet from the shore, then paddled back, stood and daringly splashed water at a young lady and the older woman with her. There was a cry of delight from the girl and one of remonstrance from the woman.

Colin noticed Fiona was watching the boats.

"Would you like t' go ont' th' water?"

"Oh, goodness, no!" Her answer was so quick it was startling.

"Miss Fiona doesn't swim," Edith put in, primly.

"Doesn't, or can't?" Colin queried.

"Can't," Fiona confirmed. "I'm afraid I've a fear of being out in a boat and having it overturn and…well, you get the idea."

"You should learn how t' swim," Colin said.

"Who'd teach me?" She laughed. "Can you swim, Mr. McCoy?"

"Very well. Me faithur took me t' th' pond behind McCoy Hall an' taught me himsel'."

He'd been around five, and the memory of actually learning to swim was dim but the image of that summer day with the sun so bright and the water so cool was still vivid. "We both stripped down an' waded in an'…"

Edith opened her little mouth to protest that kind of talk.

"I'm afraid that wouldn't be quite proper for a young lady." Fiona beat her to it.

"No, I suppose not."

Colin realized he'd be only too happy to teach Fiona how to swim if he could rid himself of Edith for a bit. Aye, find a secluded spot, get rid of all those skirts and ruffles. Just him and Fiona and nothing between them except cool water, rushing past…

"Mr. McCoy! Be careful, the horses are straying."

Fiona's little gasp brought him back. He moved his

hand, returning the horses to the path.

"Oh. Sorry. Gettin' in a bit o' daydreamin' there." He looked away, giving time for his flush to subside, to prevent Fiona from seeing it. "Would you like t' stop an' get out? We could walk on th' lake shore."

Before she could answer, another curricle came toward them from the other direction. The path, which completely encircled the lake before rejoining itself and continuing back onto the highroad, was narrow at that point, so Colin slowed the team. The top was up and he couldn't see the driver's face. The other vehicle slowed also, neared, but instead of passing, stopped alongside his.

"McCoy, hullo," came the call from inside. The driver leaned forward and a familiar face looked out at him.

"Phelan?" Colin's innards did a little flip. Fiona's other suitor here? Now? What bad luck. "Hello."

"I didn't know you an' Miss Cleary were acquainted," Phelan commented a little frigidly. His blue eyes moved past Colin to Fiona. He touched the brim of his hat courteously. "Miss Fiona."

"Why, hello, Mr. Foyle," she answered and smiled quite as if she were very glad to see him.

"We were introduced at Harrington's last week," Colin supplied. His body stiffened slightly, not liking the way she was looking at Phelan in spite of what she'd told him in the garden. He wondered if his hackles were rising and if his smile more resembled a dog's snarl.

"Oh, yes, that's right. I remember seeing you there." Phelan added, a bit reluctantly, as if he wished it hadn't been true. His accent was clear and precise, another fallen to that damned *received pronunciation*. "And got to work rather quickly, it appears."

No quicker than you, Colin thought resentfully.

As if to cover that remark before Fiona noted it, Phelan hastened on, "Is this your first time calling on Miss Fiona?"

It also seemed he was ready to establish boundaries and right of ownership.

"Would I be out with her in me curricle if it 'twas?" Colin snorted, well aware Phelan knew how these things went, just as he knew his friend hadn't gotten to the point yet where *he* might take Fiona for a drive.

Score one for th' McCoys.

"Mr. McCoy has called several times," Fiona put in, helpfully, if untruthfully.

"I see." What Phelan saw was apparently quite a bit, if the way his face darkened was any indication.

"How about you?"

"I've called only once." Phelan took a deep breath. "I see you're in a curricle." He surveyed the vehicle. "This isn't yours, is it? I seem to remember that one was a bit of a sport, with some kind of gimcrack gaudy design painted on the traces."

Colin bristled slightly, then controlled the movement. *Gimcrack indeed! As for gaudy?*

While it might've been unusual for a curricle to have any decoration, the delicate gilded patterns on its side panels had been discreet and attractive. Celtic knots, to be precise. Being Irish, Phelan should've recognized that, but perhaps he'd forgotten those along with his accent.

The curricle Colin had driven was inherited from Padraig. The knots were his brother's way of once again pointing out to Donal their Irish origins without saying a word. Since his older brother had been involved in a great many curricle races and usually insisted on driving himself everywhere, those decorations had been seen in quite a few places.

"I suppose we all have our own li'l idiosyncrasies," he said mildly. "One o' mine is honoring me ancestors with those *gaudy* designs." He stressed that one word.

Out of the corner of his eye, he saw Edith straighten and peer over the side of the curricle, searching for decoration on this one.

"Anyway…" He shrugged. "That way 'twas easy for th' spectators to know I was th' winner in a race, without askin'."

"Good-looking pair of horses." Phelan ignored that statement.

He would. Colin had beaten him in all but one race in which they competed. In that one, a set of splices in his reins had broken and he'd lost control of the team. That taught him to inspect the harness regularly.

"Those are yours, aren't they?"

"Aye. Left th' curricle, brought th' horses with me," Colin agreed.

"That reminds me, I still owe you a make-up race, for that last time when you cried foul because th' stitching came loose on your reins."

"Ah, well, that's no…"

"I say, why don't we do it now?" Phelan looked bright, and definitely eager. "That way, when I win this time, you can say it was fair and square." He glanced at Fiona. "Have you ever seen Mr. McCoy race, Miss Cleary?"

"Ah, nay, I don't think…" Colin knew damned well that challenge wasn't about a curricle race. The last thing he wanted right then was to engage in any kind of competition with his old friend and new rival.

"Your current reins are in good condition, aren't they?" Phelan pressed. "Surely those aren't the same lines you used before? Or did you bring your harness along, also?"

"Nay, this is me faithur's, but…"

A hand squeezed his bicep. Colin broke off in surprise. Fiona kept her hand where it was, not releasing the pressure.

"Go ahead," she whispered. "I'd love to see how you handle a team in a race." Louder she said, "My brother's told me of curricle races. How I'd love to see you race against Mr. McCoy, Mr. Foyle." She sighed. "I do admire a man who can handle horses."

"Then you shall," Phelan declared. "Unless you prefer to decline, Colin?"

What could he say to that? Anyway, it would be a good chance to get Phelan out of the way. Best him and show Fiona who was the superior man, the one for her.

"Nay." Colin shook his head. He looked at Fiona. "I'll help you an' Edith out."

"But I want to ride with you," she protested.

"That's definitely not going t' happen."

"But…" She looked disappointed.

"Curricle racing can be dangerous," he said, so Phelan couldn't hear. He could see his friend watching, probably thinking he was trying to wiggle out of the challenge. "I'm sure Samuel didn't tell you that." Thinking of how Lady Alisdaire had voiced that fear, he added, "Doubt if his maithur knows, aithur."

He climbed out of the curricle, calling out to a young man walking past. "Hey there, would you hold me horses while I help me lady out?"

His lady. Phelan's face went even darker.

The young man obeyed eagerly, seizing the billets of the near horse and looking at the animal enviously. Colin climbed out, released the reins and looped them over the whip. He circled behind the curricle. Edith was eager to get out. Unlike her mistress, she wanted to be nowhere near the vehicle if it was to be involved in very fast movement. She was shivering as he set her on the grass.

Colin turned back to Fiona. She was frowning. She started to speak, going to attempt to cozen him, he didn't doubt.

"Nay," he said before she could draw a breath to say the first word. "You can't ride with me, but I'll give you an important task."

"What's that?" She looked excited, and curious.

"You can be our starter." He pulled his handkerchief from his pocket, shaking it open with a flourish, and thrust it into her hand.

"What do I do?"

"Stand between th' curricles. Count t' three an' drop th' handkerchief. That'll be th' signal for the race t' begin."

"All right." She clutched the handkerchief to her bosom as if it were the most precious square of fabric in existence.

Colin wished she'd clutch him as tightly. He climbed back into the curricle and called to the youngster gripping the bits.

"Thanks. You can let go now."

The boy nodded, and having heard what he said to Fiona, immediately started shouting, "Hey, everyone.

They're going to race! Let's watch."

Immediately, there was a buzzing of conversation. Swimmers waded to shore, splashing out of the water. The boaters steered toward the dock. Young men began gathering eagerly, their companions not so much excited as curious, while the abigails, maiden aunts, and companions accompanying them dithered with disapproval. Colin immediately was struck that perhaps this wasn't such a good way to eliminate a rival. Surely, with all these older folk around, word would get back to His Lordship or Lady Alisdaire.

Nevertheless, he was more or less committed, couldn't very well back out now. He might've drawn Phelan aside and reasoned with him about postponing this until a day when he was alone, but with this many witnesses…

In the meantime, Phelan had lowered the curricle's top, then turned it around so it was facing down the path as Colin's was. His team seemed to sense something was up. They pawed and stamped, raising their heads and snorting, and he appeared to have difficulty controlling them.

Colin looked at Phelan. "What are the rules?"

"We'll ride to that big oak." Phelan pointed ahead.

About a quarter mile down the path a huge tree loomed. The base was bordered with river stones in a wide circle. The path divided, going around it.

"Circle around to the right and come back here. First one to arrive wins." He made it sound so simple.

"Good enough." Colin nodded. He glanced at Fiona. "Miss Fiona, will you do us th' honor of givin' th' signal?"

Eye shining, she nodded and walked behind his

curricle so she stood between the two vehicles. She raised her hand. A slight breeze blew off the lake, ruffling the white linen.

"One…two…"

Colin pulled his whip from its holder, tightening his grip on the reins and raising it. One of his horses pricked its ears as if he'd heard something.

"…Three…go!" Fiona dropped the handkerchief.

It fluttered to the ground and Colin flicked his whip, shaking the reins slightly. Phelan did the same and both curricles jerked forward as the horses leaped into action.

The crowd cheered.

From that moment on, Colin concentrated on his team. The horses liked to run, and once the signal was given, they burst into a leg-stretching gallop. Briefly, he and Phelan were neck-and-neck, then the bays pulled ahead.

Phelan's team caught up. Colin remembered in that fateful other race, they'd crept past his several times before the splices tore.

Damn, this is goin' t' be close.

The horses were into it wholeheartedly now, the wheels of the curricle clattering, the harness jingling and leather squeaking. The oak tree loomed ahead. He guided the team around it. Phelan somehow managed an inside turn, gaining a full head's length because of that. As they crossed behind the oak, Colin's horses had to move over or crowd Phelan's against the tree. It was close quarters and Phelan's grays moved so closely, the wheel nearest the tree seemed to spin in one spot, drilling a depression into the dirt.

The curricle tipped, overbalancing.

There was a loud groan from the spectators.

Phelan was thrown to the side, releasing the reins to grasp at the curricle's footboard. Colin automatically slowed his own team. If his friend was about to be thrown or fell out with the curricle crashing on top of him, there was a good chance he could be injured or killed. Colin's team was behind his on the turn. They might actually run over him.

A collective gasp rose from the crowd.

He guided the horses to the right, slowing even further, saw the curricle wobble and right itself. Phelan was thrown back into the seat, recovering the reins, and urging the horses forward, though they'd never slowed their momentum at all.

Someone shouted, "Yay! He's all right!"

Others echoed his words.

Colin used the whip, sending the bays leaping around the recovered curricle and the tree and onto the roadway leading back to the lake. The crowd was moving and shouting. He could hear his name as well as Phelan's being calling out by acquaintances and strangers.

Someone was standing in the center of the roadway.

Fiona.

Why the hell hadn't she moved? She was supposed to stand to the side and wave the handkerchief as they rode past, signaling the end of the race. Had he forgotten to tell her that?

Everyone else had cleared the road, making it an unobstructed way but she stood where they'd left her. The abigail was with the others, clutching her shawl and staring.

The two teams bore down on her. Colin glanced at Phelan. His friend's eyes were wide, as if he couldn't believe Fiona was standing there.

Isn't he goin' t' swerve? Surely he won't run her down. That wasn't the best way to woo a woman.

He saw Phelan's hand move, the whip rise. The horses veered to the left. Colin's own hand automatically pulled his team to the right. Edith shut her eyes tight as they thundered past. The horses galloped around Fiona.

Amid cheers and huzzahs, Colin pulled his team to a halt so quickly it raised a choking cloud of dust. Phelan's horses galloped a few yards farther before they stopped. Immediately, youngsters surged forward, but Colin wasn't watching them. He was out of the curricle, letting the reins drop, paying no mind whether the shouting congratulatory crowd was trampled by his horses or whether the team might decide to begin running again.

He ran to Fiona.

"Oh, Colin, you won! You won!" She was waving his handkerchief like a victory banner.

He ignored that. "What th' hell do you mean, standin' here? Damn it, Fiona, you could've been killed." He caught her by the shoulders, shaking her.

"Mr. McCoy!" Edith opened her eyes, giving him a startled stare. "Such language!"

He released Fiona, staggering backward. "I…I'm sorry. I mean…" He took a deep breath. "No, damn it, I'm not apologizin' You were suppose t' move. What you did was a harebrained act, an' you deserve a bit o' a tongue lashin', with curses, for endangerin' yourself so."

"Would you have been devastated if I were hurt?" She looked up at him with eyes he'd swear held stars.

"I'd have been so overwhelmed with grief I might never recover," he answered, honestly.

She continued staring at him. He took a step closer, wanting to seize her again but this time, instead of being angry, to crush his mouth against hers, and...

"All right, McCoy. I admit it, you've the better team." Phelan's declaration was like a dash of cold water.

Colin looked over his shoulder. The others, with Phelan in the lead, were watching them. Someone had caught the horses and both teams were standing placidly a few yards away.

"Told you." Colin drew in a deep breath, forcing away the curses he wanted to fling at all of them, telling them to get the hell away so he could kiss his woman in private. Instead, he held out a hand, which Phelan grasped. "Yours is a good one, however."

The crowd cheered and immediately dispersed to their own endeavors, though he heard a few discussing the race.

"Thought I'd bought it when the curricle nearly tipped." Phelan said.

Fiona shuddered delicately. "That was frightful."

"Would you have worried over me had I been injured?" he asked hopefully.

The same question she'd asked Colin.

"Perhaps paid a visit to the invalid?"

"I'd have been most concerned, Mr. Foyle," Fiona said, looking away as if even the thought upset her. "I had no idea racing was so dangerous."

"Exactly so." Phelan began to expound importantly on a theme Colin had heard him say before, to other young ladies. "That's why we like it so. Gets the blood stirring, making us feel alive."

At that moment, Colin's blood was stirring, all right,

with the desire to push his friend into his curricle and send it careening down the road and out of sight while he shouted after it, *I won. Get out o' here!*

Perhaps Phelan sensed this. He caught Fiona's hand, bowing over it, then tipped his hat.

"I'll be going now. May I still visit you this coming Monday, Miss Fiona?" There was an uncertainty in his voice, as if he realized Colin had won more than a mere race.

"I shall look forward to it, Mr. Foyle." While Colin stared, she actually fluttered her eyelashes at Phelan and squeezed his fingers slightly.

"At ten, then." Phelan gently withdrew his gloved hand from hers. With a quick glance at Colin's darkening expression, he returned to the curricle.

Colin waited until his friend was on his way before he spoke.

"You were flirtin' with him."

"No, I wasn't."

"You were. *I'd have been most concerned…I'll look forward t' it…*" He mimicked her words. "You gave him butterfly eyes!" he accused. "An' pressed his fingers. How could you say aloud you were eager for him t' come calling with me standin' here?"

"Well, he *is* my suitor, too…"

"Nay. He *isn't* your suitor," Colin raised his voice, realized a few heads turned in their direction, and spoke quieter. "*I* am."

He caught her arm, shaking her.

"I'll remind you what you said in th' garden. You're me woman, Fiona, an' if you think ithirwise, you'd better do a serious bit o' reconsiderin'."

She didn't answer. Her expression was so startled he

was certain she'd never believed he'd react in such a way. It seemed to say she might've spoken out of hand that day.

"Well?"

"It's true I care for you, Mr. McCoy."

She could've argued, he realized, pointed out they'd only seen each other a total of three times, and he'd made no commitment or declaration either she or her family might consider that ultimate and final one. She might've said what she told him was made in the heat of his emotional declaration and that kiss. Instead, she simply stared at him, the color leeching slowly from her face.

"Then you'd better think on that, an' come t' a decision about Phelan Foyle before he shows up on Monday." Colin forced himself not to feel pity at her expression. He pushed her toward the curricle while little Edith fairly goggled. "I think I'd better take you home."

"But…"

"No buts." He didn't let her finish. "You're goin' home. T' ponder."

****

Colin left Fiona and her maid at Alisdaire Manor's front door.

"Give me apologies t' your maithur." He reminded himself to be polite and make his excuses, wondering what Fiona would tell her parents.

He was well aware that, no matter how she felt about him, if she related his words at the lake, with or without adding the incident of the race, they might consider him unacceptable son-in-law material and forbid his setting foot inside Alisdaire Manor again.

"I shall see you this Monday t' hear what you've decided."

"Monday? But that's the day Mr. Foyle is coming to call." Fiona protested. "Surely if the two of you are here at the same time…"

"Depends on how long one o' us stays. Tomorrow's Sunday. I suggest you use it t' severely meditate." With that, he tipped his hat, climbed back into the curricle, gathered the reins, and drove away without a backward glance.

"Oh, Miss." Edith watched the curricle disappear down the drive. "He's terrible handsome when he's angry, ain't he?"

"Yes, Edith." Fiona breathed the words as if she couldn't speak any louder. "He most certainly is."

"What are you going to do?"

"The only thing I can." She didn't elaborate. "After all, I've been given an ultimatum, haven't I?"

Edith didn't answer. Instead, she opened the door and they went inside.

"Back so early?" Lady Alisdaire stood in the foyer, looking past Fiona in concern. "Where's Mr. McCoy? I was going to invite him to stay for elevenses. We're having cream tea today."

"I'm afraid Mr. McCoy remembered he had urgent business to attend and thus cut our drive short." Fiona looked away, putting fingers to her mouth. Briefly, her lips trembled.

"Fiona, dear." Her mother put a hand on her arm. "Is everything all right?"

"Everything's fine, Mamma." Fiona turned a too-bright smile on her. "You said, elevenses? Is it that time all ready? Goodness, I do believe I'm famished. All that fresh lake air…"

She hurried away to the parlor where a morning high

tea had been laid.

"Perhaps it's a good thing Mr. McCoy didn't stay. I'm certain he'd be embarrassed by the appetite I'm about to display."

Only Edith saw her wipe her fingers across the tear on her cheek as she hurried to the parlor.

Chapter 11

Colin arrived at Alisdaire Manor at half past ten, not wanting to meet Phelan Foyle that particular day.

He failed in that respect. As he dismounted at the iron hitching post, he saw Phelan's chestnut tied there and his friend being ushered out by Hilton—*or perhaps former friend,* he thought, as he saw the crestfallen and darkened expression.

Colin met him on the flagstone to the front steps. Briefly, they regarded each other in silence. A moment of doubt crept in. What if Fiona had chosen his rival who was now leaving so he wouldn't witness Colin's own embarrassment?

"You win again." Phelan thrust out his hand. "This time, there won't be a rematch, will there?"

Colin didn't answer. At that point, there was nothing he could say which wouldn't sound like gloating. Relief flooding through him, he didn't hesitate to grasp Phelan's hand.

"She's a lovely lass, Col." There was something in Phelan's expression telling Colin he'd actually cared for Fiona, that his attempted courtship wasn't merely a duty to wed an heiress. "Be good to her."

"Be assured I will." Colin released his hand.

With a nod, Phelan continued down the path to his horse. Colin didn't move until he had mounted and ridden away. Then, he continued to the manor where

Hilton, seeing his arrival, waited with the door still open.

"Good morning, Mr. McCoy." The butler stepped back to allow him entry.

"Good morning, Hilton." Colin removed his hat and the butler took it along with his gloves. "Miss Fiona's expectin' me, I believe."

Best to pretend he knew nothing of what had been said between her and Phelan, which was in part true because he had no idea how she'd gone about telling him he was the loser in the courtship game.

"Yes, sir, she's in the garden," came the reply. "If you'll come this way?"

He was led through the house to the door opening into the little courtyard where that momentous first tea had been held, where now Fiona sat on a stone bench down the path.

Today, she was wearing a morning gown of some light fabric, cream-colored and sprigged with embroidered green leaves and rosebuds. She didn't look at him as he walked toward her, though he knew she was aware, had heard his footsteps on the flagstones.

Any other time he would've greeted her with a compliment about her gown. Today, he stopped before her, not speaking. She seemed to be contemplating one of the trees beyond the garden wall. Thinking perhaps of their mild adventure at the brook?

Briefly, she didn't move, didn't acknowledge his presence. At last, as if she could ignore him no longer, she turned her head, looked up at him, and stood.

"I did as you asked."

It was an admission more of defeat than anything else, he thought, and he really hadn't wanted that. He wanted her happy in her choice, not as if she were bowing to his will.

"It broke his heart a bit, I think, if the way he took it was any indication."

"He wasn't abusive?" Even with the pity he felt for Phelan, if he'd said or made any threat in anger…

"Oh, no. He was a gentleman. As always."

Was there a hint that he wasn't? Colin didn't respond.

"Wished me well. Thanked me…for what exactly, I'm not sure…and took his leave."

"I saw him as I arrived."

"You didn't have words?" Again, he wasn't certain if her concern was for him or Phelan.

"We shook hands an' parted as much friends as possible."

"Good."

"Fiona…" For the first time, Colin wondered if the way he'd gone about this was all wrong. "If you…" He forced himself to say it. "If there's any doubt in your mind, o' how you feel about Phelan Foyle…or me, for that matter, tell me. Now."

"There is none."

She sighed and he thought it was the relief of shedding a burden, getting past a difficult decision. She looked up at him.

"I love you, Colin McCoy, and I've made my choice." She laughed slightly. "I hope I've made the right one."

"Why would you say that?"

"Because I have this fear you're going to tell me you've simply been playing with my heart, as I tried to play with yours. I guess I can admit it now, can't I? For a short time, I let the thought of having two suitors go to my head. Now that I've turned Phelan away, are you going to walk out?"

"Don't you trust me?"

"That's just it. I do…but there's always a bit of doubt clinging, I suppose, when one does something so momentous."

He didn't answer.

"What happens now, Colin?"

"Now? I'll show you."

With that, he bowed, turned, and walked away.

"Wait," she called after him. "Where are you going?"

"There's somethin' I must do." He looked back, seeing she was about to follow. "Stay there. Wait for me."

He went into the house.

Luckily, Hilton was passing the doors.

"Hilton."

The butler paused, looking back. "Yes, Mr. McCoy?"

"Would you ask if I might have a word with His Lordship?"

A flicker of interest touched the butler's face. "Certainly, sir. He's in his study. If you'll wait here?"

In the longest ten minutes of Colin's life, Hilton disappeared down the hallway, then, in a few moments, returned.

"This way, sir." He led Colin to Alisdaire's study, announced him, and went on his way.

"You want to see me, boy?" Alisdaire was his usual gruff but vague self.

"Yes, sir, I…"

"Been quite a bit of activity around here this

morning. Some other young man coming and going. He didn't stay long either. Are you come to say goodbye before you leave? *He* didn't."

"No, sir." Colin looked around. His Lordship hadn't gotten up from his desk. It wouldn't do for him to continue standing, looking down at him. "May I sit, sir?"

"By all means. That's what that chair's for." Alisdaire seemed to find that comment amusing. He often appeared to think his own words held humor when no one else did.

He waited until Colin was settled, though that really couldn't be the proper term because he was perched on the edge of the chair, ramrod-straight and not relaxed at all.

"You've something to tell me, I think? Or ask, perhaps I should say?"

"Yes, sir. Both." Colin took an extra second to compose his thoughts. Everything he'd rehearsed on the ride over went completely out of his head. *Just as well*, he thought. *Perhaps this should come directly from me heart an' not be a speech drafted an' memorized.*

Taking a deep breath, he plunged in.

"Your Lordship, as you know, I've called on Miss Fiona several times now."

"Twice to be exact," his Lordship supplied.

"An' I hope you've observed I've developed an abidin' affection for her."

"Actually, I imagine my wife would have done more of the observing," Alisdaire corrected. "Since she's been the one here more when you were in attendance."

"Yes, well, anyway…I know what I wish t' say may be cuttin' across the usual rules of conduct where this type o' social interaction is concerned…"

"Good God, boy. Can't you say anything in letters of less than four syllables?"

"Sir?"

"I hope I'm correct in surmising where this is heading, so let me save us both some trouble and ask you a few questions."

"Certainly, sir."

"Can you provide for my daughter?"

"I believe so, sir. As I told you, I'm clerkin' for me faithur, so I won't be livin' on th' family fortune." Colin made a mental note to speak to Quinton about doing exactly that when he returned home. "As a third son, I'm not th' principal heir anyway, but I will inherit a substantial bit. I've a good character, not like me braithur Padraig…"

Colin hesitated. Best not to mention Padraig, perhaps.

"We've already been over that, I think." Alisdaire agreed. "I'm well aware you're not that rapscallion. Been a fairly quiet boy, haven't you?" The old man gave him a wink. "Not too quiet, I hope. Don't want you to be dull. Do you have a mistress?"

"No sir. I ne'er have, an' don't plan ta." Perhaps that was a bit too vehement. *Will he think I'm protestin' too much?*

"Good. They can become expensive. I wouldn't want you spending coin on some ladybird that you could better use elsewhere. I suppose that means you've no byblows to siphon off whatever fortune you inherit, either?"

He didn't miss Colin's flush, and that seemed to entertain him.

"I assure you, sir, whatever dalliances I've had have

been unfruitful ones." Colin drew himself up even straighter in the chair. He wasn't about to let this conversation go any further. It was embarrassing and he might soon say something he'd regret. "I believe you know how I feel about Miss Fiona, an' I don't think we need t' question me character any further. All that needs to be said is this: Will you allow me th' privilege o' askin' your daughter t' be me wife?"

"Well now, that's direct enough. Why couldn't you say that sooner?"

"Does that mean you give your permission?"

"What if I don't?"

"Then I'm afraid we'll be elopin', sir."

"Not if I have anything to do with it."

There was a long silence broken only when Alisdaire laughed.

"Well? Are you going to sit there staring at me, or get yourself to the garden and ask her? Go, boy! I'll officially get in touch with your father about the arrangements later this week."

"Thank you, sir." Colin bolted out of the chair as if he'd been stung by a bee. Pushing open the doors, he sent them crashing shut behind him before His Lordship finished speaking.

****

Colin made his way through the hallways back to the garden doors. Fiona was where he'd left her, sitting disconsolately on the bench. At some point she'd picked a rose, then proceeded to demolish it, plucking the petals in a game of *he-loves-me-he-loves-me-not*, then worrying each one into small pieces now littering her skirt and the space around the bench in bright pink shreds.

As he approached, she spun around on the bench. He thought she looked disbelieving. Had she really thought he'd abandoned her, playing some cruel game costing her a more sincere suitor, before he deserted her?

Colin dismissed that thought. Whether she did or nay, whether she didn't love him as much as he loved her…it would work itself out in time, he was sure.

Before she could speak, he pulled the stem of the mutilated rose from her fingers, tossed it away, seized her hand, and dropped onto the bench beside her. He turned her hand over and kissed the palm, then each of her fingers.

"Mr. McCoy? What are you doing?" She tried to pull her hand from his, looking around hastily to make certain none of the servants or possibly one of her parents was around to witness the unexpected intimacy he'd just performed.

"Settin' th' stage, Miss Fiona." He pressed her palm against his chest, hoping she could feel the pounding of his heart through the linen. "Miss Fiona…nay, I'll dispense with that now…Fiona, me darlin', me love, will you do me th' honor o' becomin' me wife?"

She stared at him, mouth dropping open.

"Say *yes*," he whispered. "So I'll be free t' make love t' you as I've wanted since th' night we met."

"M-my father…"

"Aye, he's agreeable. That's where I went. Well?"

"Y-yes, Mr. Mc-…Colin…" Her words were as soft as his. "I will."

"Thank God!"

With that, he pulled her to him, pressing his mouth to hers in a deep, harsh, invasive kiss. His lips crushed against her own, tongue seeking. Fiona took a deep breath, stiffened, then went soft and pliant against him. Her own hands crept timidly up his shoulders, then abruptly, almost convulsively, tightened. When Colin released her, they were both visibly trembling.

"Best stop now before I cause a scandal," he muttered.

"When…"

"I'll leave th' details o' th' wedding t' your faithur," he replied. "As long as 'tis soon."

"I meant…" She shook her head. "When are you going to make love to me?"

"Oh, Lord, lass! Right now if I had me way, but…'twill be after th' wedding when we're legally bound, else I'll mire us both in gossip, because once I start havin' carnal knowledge o' you, I'm ne'er goin' t' stop."

This time, it was she who began the kiss, and while it was a bit inexpert, it was almost as arousing to him as his own had been.

"Good," she whispered. "Because I'm never going to want you to stop, either."

"Oh, God, I'm glad t' hear you say that." His words were a groan.

Colin released her, pushing her away and sliding to the far end of the bench.

"Sit there," he ordered. "Don't come within reach, else I may forget meself."

God in Heaven…I'm goin' t' be married, his mind screamed, while his heart sighed with soft anticipation.

Chapter 12

A few hours later, Colin returned home. After more soft words and—even to his mind—scandalous promises and the decision they should adjourn to the manor house and seek the company of Lord and Lady Alisdaire and make everything official, which included having a celebratory tea in the parlor, he bade farewell to his intended and his future in-laws, and was on his way back to McCoy Hall.

Instead of going in directly, however, he rode his horse to the stables where he proceeded to unsaddle and tend the animal himself, much to the groom's consternation.

"You're not satisfied with how I've been handlin' your horses, sir?" he asked.

"Nay, as far as I'm concerned, you're a gem among grooms," Colin replied. "In fact, I couldn't ask for a better man t' care for me animals. 'Tis just that t'day, I feel th' need for a little introspection, an' tendin' t' me horse seemed th' best way to handle it."

Satisfied with that explanation, the groom took the saddle and bridle to be put away, leaving Colin to his task. Once the horse was curried and rubbed down and placed in his stall, he proceeded to the house, though perhaps his *introspection* hadn't progressed very far.

****

"May I interrupt, sir?"

Quinton was in his study, still struggling through the accounts. When he saw Colin hovering in the doorway, he waved him inside.

"Still not likin' those thin's a bit better, Da?"

"Nay, an' I'm ready t' get serious about hirin' mesel' a clerk t' save me mind."

"About that…"

"Aye?"

"You'd mentioned t' me that you'd appreciate me assistance. If you still wish it, I'll be glad t' take on th' duty."

"As much as I'd be most thankful, lad, I'm a tad suspicious." Quinton cocked his head to one side and regarded his youngest. "Why have you changed your mind? Last time I broached th' subject, you were adamant in showin' no interest."

"I've thought on it an' decided 'twas selfish of me not t' help you, sir, especially when you've done so much for me. Besides, 'tis time I put some o' me education t' use, don't you think?"

"In that case, I'll accept your offer, an' you can start right now, afore you change your mind." Quinton was up from behind the desk, ushering Colin around it and settling him in the chair. He pushed the open ledger toward him. "Here's this month's accounts."

His father was out of the study before Colin could utter a word. Sighing, he studied the page with its rows of numbers entered in black or red ink. He was glad he was at least familiar with the various farms and villages and had been around them enough with Quinton that he could easily understand what the notations meant.

He managed to dally with the accounts until it was time for supper. Quinton always required they dress for the evening meal, so Geoffrey already had his evening clothes laid out when he got to his room.

"You seem agitated, sir." Leave it to the valet to notice. "Color's a bit high. You aren't comin' down with somethin', are you?" He frowned. "I haven't heard o' any ailments goin' round th' villages."

"Nay, just a bit winded from th' ride home, I imagine," Colin brushed his concern aside, changing the subject. "I'm thinking I want a bit o' color t'night." He picked up the black satin waistcoat lying on the bed. "Change this for that red silk one with th' gold embroidery."

****

Colin came down to dinner resplendent. Màiri complimented him on his appearance, as did Felicity. Even Donal noticed, frowning slightly as if he also thought his younger brother a bit flushed, though he didn't mention it.

Once their father was at table and preparing to give his usual summary of the news before starting the meal, Colin got to his feet so quickly, he seemed to have been prodded.

"Colin, what in th' world?" his father exclaimed.

"Da...Mama..." He bowed to each and glanced at Donal. "E'eryone. I've somethin' t' say afore you tell us o' t'day's newsworthy events."

"Can't it wait?" Quinton obviously didn't like someone, even one of his sons, stealing this little moment of limelight from him.

"It could, but I'd prefer it not, sir."

"By all means..." Quinton sat down, with an acquiescent, if somewhat ironical, gesture. "If 'tis more important than th' fact o' that Nightingale woman openin' a trainin' school for female nurses at St. Thomas's, or our colonists in New Zealand fightin' those Maori or whatever they're called, or that th' dictator of Italy is marchin' against Messina…well, by all means, me son, go ahead. Please."

"Thank you, sir." Ignoring his father's sarcasm, Colin bowed deferentially. "Once I say it, you'll admit this is o' more importance, sir…at least t' me…an' perhaps t' our family." He paused.

"Well," Donal burst out. "What is it? Get on with it, Col. Don't stop now."

"I've been given permission by Lord Alisdaire t' ask his daughter t' marry me." Colin made his announcement so quietly everyone leaned forward as if they couldn't hear.

"An'?" Quinton prompted.

"An'…I've done so."

"An'?" his father asked again.

"An' she accepted me proposal."

"Thank God for that," With a gusty sigh, Quinton leaned back in his chair. "I'd hate t' think th' McCoys had been insulted by that slip o' a lass."

"Sir, speak kindly. That slip o' a lass will soon be your daughter-in-law." Colin stifled a smirk.

"Isn't this a bit of a rush?" Màiri put in. "I mean, you've only just met th' girl a fortnight ago an' seen her…how many times?"

"Enough t' know, Mama, an' afore you e'en dare think it…there's no scandal attached t' me proposal. I've been quite circumspect. I'm simply in love."

He sat down and picked up his napkin, unfolding it and tucking it into his shirtfront.

"Well now." Quinton stood. "I agree. All ithir news

seems anticlimactic compared t' this. Cormac, bring out me best wine. We need t' drink a toast t' me boy here."

Màiri began to sniffle, but Quinton quelled any tears.

"Save them for th' wedding, m'dear. Now's a time t' celebrate, not cry." He laughed as Cormac reappeared and began to serve the goblets on a small silver tray.

Chapter 13

Time seemed to fly after that, fast enough to make Colin's head spun. Fast enough not to give him time to think of what was coming and perhaps get panic-stricken and want to take a dash.

A few days after his announcement, Lord Alisdaire came to call. He was closeted with Quinton for several hours, calmly forbidding Colin entrance. When he protested, Alisdaire opened the study door, said, "You may be the one marrying, but I'm the one who'll be footing the bill for this wedding," and shut the door again.

Colin had no answer to that. His Lordship was correct. As father of the bride, he'd pay for Fiona's wedding dress, the pre-bridal dinner for all the guests who'd be staying at Alisdaire Manor and McCoy Hall, and the decorating of the church, as well as Fiona's dowry.

The dowry. Colin hadn't even thought of that.

He wondered how much money Alisdaire was handing over to him for the privilege of marrying his daughter…and would he see any of it? The reception and wedding banquet would be held at McCoy Hall, so perhaps Quinton might claim the dowry as his due for supplying a place for guests to congratulate the newly wedded couple, as well as where they would spend their first night as husband and wife. The McCoy hunting lodge had been suggested for the wedding night, in such a way as to leave Colin no room for refusal.

The banns were posted and Fiona and her mother, with Màiri in attendance, set about composing a guest list, surprising Colin by asking the names of people he'd wish to invite. He mumbled a couple of names and let it go at that. Truly, he hadn't thought of asking any of his college chums to be witness to his tying the knot. The ladies wrangled over the menus and decorations. Fiona had numerous appointments with the dressmaker and as many crises in selecting dress style and colors for herself and her bridal attendants, while Colin languished alone in Alisdaire Manor's parlor making small talk with Her Ladyship until she returned.

Somewhere in the midst of all the hubbub, Colin and Fiona had a moment alone to decide on their wedding trip. She wanted Paris. He, in spite of having seen that city as well as quite a few others on his Grand Tour, agreed. To Colin, one city was as good as another, since if he had his way, they wouldn't set foot outside the bedroom long enough to see much of it. Anyway, he'd gotten only a glimpse that other time because his father was along.

Shortly after the betrothal was formally announced at a party at Alisdaire Manor, Donal and Felicity returned to London. Donal promised they'd be back for the wedding.

"Do you think I'd miss such an event?" He winked, then appeared startled that he'd broken his usual staid manner to do such a frivolous thing. "Besides, Father and Mother would be disappointed if the entire family isn't here."

But the entire family won't be here, Colin thought.

Padraig won't be here. He wondered if Quinton had bothered to notify Padraig, decided he'd do so himself, and to that end, seated himself at the writing desk in his bedchamber and composed a letter he gave to Geoffrey to post.

****

Padraig Aloysius Francis McCoy, Esquire
The Shamrock Ranch
McCoy's Crossing, Nebraska Territory
United States of America
My dear brother,

I'm sure you're surprised to receive a letter from me after all these years. Father never forbade me to write but I suppose I simply had nothing to say until now.

Well, on with it. I'm being married soon, to Lord Alisdaire's daughter, Fiona. I think you might remember her. Samuel Cleary's sister? That skinny little lass who cried that time Samuel caught a frog and showed it to her. She's no longer little, nor skinny, and she's won my heart. When I realized that, I saw I had two choices, to be as unrestrained as you in showing the lass how I felt, or marrying her. I'm not you, Padraig—though occasionally I wish I had more of your vinegar—so I opted for marriage.

By the time you receive this letter I'll be a seasoned veteran of the marriage bed. Be happy for me, Brother, and know you are often in my thoughts.

Your loving brother,
Coilin Uilliam Conchobher McCoy
McCoy Hall
Tipperary, Ireland
The United Kingdom of Great Britain

Chapter 14

Time for the wedding drew closer. Donal and Felicity returned. Within the next days, the house would soon be filled with relatives and other invited guests.

As the day approached, Colin became predictably nervous. Surprisingly, Donal began paying him attention, offering comforting words that were astoundingly soothing. They made Colin wonder if his brother had gone through the same thing before his own marriage. He'd been too young at that time to care about premarital jitters, and now was curious who, if anyone, had offered calming phrases to Donal.

They were at dinner, the last one they would have as a family before the horde of guests descended. Quinton delivered the evening news, as usual.

"First an' foremost, I've had a letter from our distant relative." That was the way he now referred to Padraig, rarely mentioning his middle son by name.

****

Padraig was now working as a cowboy at a ranch in a little town called Four Corners.

A letter had arrived several years before, relating how his employer had been killed during a cattle drive when the herd stampeded. Padraig had taken the remittance money sent him faithfully every month and bought his late owner's ranch, changing the name from the Circle-J to the Shamrock. He also stated this now made him what westerners called a *cattle baron*. Later, a second letter came, telling of an influenza epidemic in which he'd saved the town by riding through snow to the next town over and bringing back a doctor. Shortly afterward, the Four Corners council changed the name of their little town to McCoy's Crossing.

Quinton admitted skepticism at all this.

"Sounds like some penny-dreadful tale t' me," he'd muttered. Nevertheless, they saw a flicker of pride behind his words.

****

Colin wondered if perhaps Padraig received the letter he'd sent and was replying, although it seemed not enough time had passed for it to cross the Atlantic and travel to Nebraska and another make its way back along the same route. Anyway, would his father open a letter not addressed to him?

Quinton followed his current introduction to Padraig's most recent letter with, "I have t' say what this letter contains was a shock."

At her place, Màiri drew in a sharp breath. Her fingers tightened around her napkin.

"You needn't worry, me dear," Quinton saw the movement. "There hasn't been another o' those stampedes, an' th' boy hasn't been harmed."

Padraig was now close to three-and-thirty, but Quinton always called him *the boy* and probably always would.

"But he's done a most surprisin' an', t' my way o' thinkin', questionable thing." He paused.

"What is it?" Donal burst out as the silence deepened. "If he wasn't hurt in a stampede, has he been in one of those gunfights? Was he scalped by an Indian?"

129

"Let me read part o' it t' you." Quinton let that sentence hang in the air while he picked up the letter he'd placed by his plate.

Clearing his throat, he opened it.

It began with the customary greeting, which Quinton read without a quaver.

Quinton Aloysius Francis Xavier McCoy, Esquire
McCoy Hall
Tipperary, Ireland
The United Kingdom of Great Britain
Honored Father,
Please forgive this influx of letters I've sent you recently but many things have occurred of which I wish you to be aware.

"Well now, don't know as I'd call three letters in six years an influx…" Quinton muttered. He harrumphed loudly, "Where was I? Oh, yes…" and resumed.

…many things have occurred of which I wish you to be aware.

Another incident has happened, and while I'm certain this will shock you, be assured I am even more shaken by it.

Father, I have taken a wife.

I must make that a single and solitary statement on this page, for it deserves to stand alone in its uniqueness. Surely you see the irony here? After all my womanizing and playing fast and loose with many females' hearts, my own has been captured and is now held prisoner.

Her name is Maria and she's from Alta California, a territory in the far western part of the country originally settled by the Spanish. She's gently bred, a lady, and…I fear you will laugh at me, Father, for I find there is not enough foolscap in the world to hold all the words I need to extol her virtues or describe how I feel about her. Yes, sir, I have fallen, very violently and permanently.

Please be happy for me, sir, and give me your blessings in this foray I am about to make into the totally uncharted waters of being a husband.

Convey this news to my mother and my siblings, and also give them my affection.

Speaking of marriage, sir, did my older brother ever get himself to the altar? It's been some ten years now since his betrothal to that lass from London was announced. I read of it before I left the country.

At that, Donal started slightly, as if even now he was shaken by the fact that Padraig had been in London during his courting of Felicity, though he hadn't been certain of it.

Your son,
Padraig Aloysius Francis McCoy
The Shamrock Ranch
McCoy's Crossing, Nebraska Territory
United States of America

Quinton looked up, laying down the letter.

"You mean he's never been informed Felicity and I are married?" Donal burst out. "Father, you *do* respond occasionally, don't you?"

"Aye," Quinton admitted. "But only mostly t' acknowledge receipt o' his letters. Never relaying anything o' personal import."

"Well, I think you should relay this personal import as soon as possible." Donal was plainly shaken out of his usual calm.

"Now, Donal…" Felicity placed a soothing hand on his arm. "It isn't such a terrible thing."

"No? My own father doesn't acknowledge our marriage to my brother who thinks we're still betrothed, or possibly worse, after nearly a decade?"

"Oh, dear." Felicity now looked shocked. "You don't think he might believe we're…living in sin?"

Colin stifled a snicker at that.

"Who knows what Padraig thinks?" Donal retorted. "*I* never did."

"You're right, son. I'll notify him in my next letter, or perhaps you'd care t' do it yourself?" Quinton looked hopeful.

Donal shook his head and didn't answer.

"I must say this deflates my sails a bit," Colin spoke up. "I sincerely hope you're not going t' announce this news t' anyone else, Da."

Quinton looked at him questioningly.

"Not that I don't want people t' know…but, well…I took it upon meself t' write Padraig o' me own marriage an' now he sends this. 'Tis as if he's trying t' one-up me. An'…call me selfish, but I don't want anythin' detractin' from me own weddin' day."

He flushed as he said it, feeling somehow disloyal to Padraig while ambiguously angry at the same time.

"You're right, lad." Quinton didn't have to think about it. "I won't mention Padraig unless someone asks, an' then I'll simply make it a flat statement an' go on."

"Thank you, Da," Colin muttered. He lifted his goblet and took a swallow to hide his flush.

"Was there other news?" Màiri broke in, attempting to gloss over this unusual show of petty emotion by her youngest.

"Nay," Quinton answered. "I don't think anythin' can be o' as much import as that I've just reported."

"Guess that puts me in me own place, doesn't it?" Colin muttered, knowing he was acting like a pouting brat and not caring a bit.

"Now, lad…"

"Let's drink a toast," Donal got to his feet also. He raised his glass. "Two of them. To Colin…and to that far-distant relative."

Colin drank but told himself he was saluting his own marriage and not Padraig's. Supper seemed rather anticlimactic after that.

Later, in the drawing room, with Colin and Donal supplied with glasses of brandy, Quinton unleased his paternal fury at his second son.

"How can he do that?" he railed. "Get married?"

"Now, Da…" Surprisingly, it was Donal who tried to calm Quinton. "If Padraig were still here, wouldn't you be trying to settle him with a wife?"

"Aye, but…he'd be where I could keep an eye on him. Do you suppose any o' those people in that li'l town know o' his past? How many wives is he diddlin' there while they're namin' that town after him?"

"From all I've heard, the West is where men go to relieve themselves of their past reputations and build new ones," Donal commented. "Perhaps Padraig has done that. You said yourself his letters show a change."

"He's bought a ranch," Colin put in. "He's a landowner now, responsible for ithirs. Like you are, Da."

He hoped that comparison might quiet Quinton a bit. He also hoped it showed he wasn't jealous of his brother. Colin was still shaken a bit by his own reaction to Padraig's letter.

"He risked his life ridin' t' that ithir town t' fetch th' doctor when that epidemic came through…an' they did change th' name o' their town t' honor him for that. It sounds as if he's really mended his ways, Da."

"Aye, *sounds like*, but has he really? You may not remember, Colin, but I know *you* do, Donal. How Padraig could always look so innocent while devisin' th' most dev'lish schemes." Quinton shook his head. "All I can think o' is that poor girl. Does she really know what she's gettin' into? Alta California? Where th' hell is that, anyway? He said she's Spanish. She's probably some sheltered li'l thin' from a convent who's flattered by all th' attention he's givin' her, an'…"

"Well, what do you intend t' do?" Colin burst out. "Board a ship an' sail t' America? Go stormin' t' Padraig's ranch an' tell his wife what a dastardly scoundrel her husband is? For all you know, he isn't that way now…an' the fact he's taken a wife proves it. For God's sake, let it go, Da. Anyway, they're already married an' what's done is done. If Padraig's still stickin' t' his old ways or if he's reformed, it's her problem, not yours! You should simply stay out o' it."

Quinton stared at him, and Colin was startled by his own boldness at speaking so to his father.

"Da, I'm sorry, I…"

"Nay, you're right." Quinton's reply was quiet and agreeing. "Whate'er he does now, I simply have t' have faith that what he's been tellin' me isn't lies but th' truth." He looked up and forced a smile. "Let's have anaithur toast. Donal, pour us a glass. No need t' bother Cormac."

As his son obeyed, bringing the decanter to them, Quinton seized his glass and raised it. "To me sons…all o' them… Two are makin' me proud. God grant th' ithir is also, sight unseen."

Later, when all had retired and the house was quiet, Quinton opened the left middle drawer of his desk. It was always kept locked, and he now took the key from his watch chain and opened the drawer.

Inside were the letters Padraig had sent him, arranged with the latest on top. He took out the last letter, opening it and reading again the lines where Padraig related how he'd ridden his horse forty miles through a blizzard to get a doctor from the neighboring city of Lancaster and bring him back to treat the ailing inhabitants of Four Corners. Padraig himself was overcome by the cold and exposure and the disease causing the deaths of several people. When he recovered, it was to discover the townsfolk, in gratitude, had changed the name of the town to McCoy's Crossing, after the man who'd saved so many of them at risk of his own life.

...Now I must ask you a question. I was ill in probably mid-November. Father, did you think of me during that time? I ask because in my delirium, I swear I heard you speaking, lamenting your failure where I was concerned. Whether you did think of me or if this was simply the ravings of a feverish mind, I wish you to know you did not fail, sir. You were merely the instrument delivering me from the ill influence of my surroundings into the place where I might become the man I should be. Be assured I am no longer the scoundrel who called himself your son but have taken on the mantle of respectability.

I hope should anyone now enquire of me you will inform them with some pride that I am a prosperous businessman, wellliked by the community in which he lives. I owe my present condition to you, Father, and, where I once lamented your ultimatum, now I am grateful for it…

The letter fell to the desk. Quinton sat there for some time, staring at the single sheet of paper, at the creases where it was folded to form an envelope. Gently he closed the letter, running his fingers down the edges.

"Ah, Padraig…I wish you were here, lad, so I could tell you how often I do think o' you."

He returned the letter to the drawer, taking this newest one and placing it on top. Then he shut the drawer, locked it, and returned the key to his watch chain.

Chapter 15

It was the eve of the wedding. The family had returned from the rehearsal at the church, Colin fidgeting impatiently while the priest told them where to stand and when to reply during the ceremony. Amid blushes and many glances thrown his way, Fiona and her friends giggled and laughed. Occasionally, one would whisper something and Fiona's face would turn bright pink and that brought more laughter.

Colin was tired of the entire thing and wished it was over, the celebrating done, and he and Fiona at the lodge, snuggled in the down-mattressed feather bed with no one around for miles. No one except Geoffrey and Edith, who'd be going with them, of course, and the driver of the coach and the footman. Once, while Reverend Hennessey was explaining something, he'd leaned toward Fiona and whispered, "Lass, what say we elope t'night?"

That brought first a shocked look, then as if she were seriously considering the idea.

Colin shook his head. "Nay, 'twould disappoint your parents an' me maithur too much, I'm thinkin'. Guess I can put up with a few more hours o' this."

He hoped.

Back again at McCoy Hall, everyone was in a cheerful mood, supper was elegant and delicious, and Quinton's wine flowed like water. Many toasts were made.

Donal gave a surprisingly heartfelt speech wishing Fiona and Colin much happiness, though there was something about his expression bothering Colin a bit, as if he meant something other than he was saying.

Colin made his own speech as he presented his betrothed with her wedding gift, a pearl-and-diamond brooch that had belonged to his grandmother Cuilline. Màiri had given it to him that morning. Fiona likewise presented Colin with a gold watch fob in the shape of a heart. On closer examination he discovered it to be a locket and upon opening it, he found the bottom section of the heart was actually a daguerreotype bearing Fiona's likeness.

"Lass, I'll wear this on me watch chain an' when'er I check th' time, I'll think o' you," he declared. If they'd been in a more private place, he'd have kissed the image and her also, but they weren't, so he promised himself, *later*…

By the time Colin's college chums, his male cousins, and Donal swept him away for yet another party, this one wisely not mentioned to the older guests but one the men were of course well aware of, they were all a bit foxed because Quinton hadn't stinted on bringing out his best wine for the occasion.

"Where are we goin'?" Colin demanded as he clambered onto his horse, aided a bit by Donal giving him a leg up.

"Secret," his brother replied. "You'll know when we get there."

This particular party had been arranged by Phelan Foyle, who was invited to the wedding and had been a guest at the supper also. Colin questioned the propriety of that invitation, and when Donal told him Phelan wished to host his bachelor send-off, he'd been even more doubtful.

"Nay, I don't think so…" Colin began his refusal, only to have Phelan interrupt.

"I'd truly like to do this, Col."

"Not t' put too fine a point on it, Phey, but don't you think it a wee bit in bad taste t' have me future wife's rejected suitor hostin' th' to-do given for me final night as a single man?"

"Why?" Phelan laughed. "Do you think I'm going to try some grand scheme of revenge? Get you drunk and leave you floating naked in the town fountain for the entire world to see?" He aimed a gentle fist at Colin's shoulder. "Don't believe I didn't think of that. Then I realized how petty that would make me. We're friends, Col, and friends won't let a thing like rivalry over a lass come betwixt them."

He looked at Donal, who was standing to one side with an amused expression.

"Donal, tell him. I want to do this to establish once and for all we're still friends."

"In that case, all right," Colin agreed, ignoring the twinge in his belly cautioning he might be making a mistake. "But be warned, Phelan Foyle." He shook a finger. "If you're playin' me false, I'll come after you an' do whate'er you do t' me twice o'er!"

"Agreed!" Phelan stuck out his hand. Colin seized it. "You'll see," he promised. "This will be a party to end all nuptial parties."

That little talk ended with Colin asking Phelan to be one of his groomsmen, also.

The party was held at Madame DeLancey's, the

most famous, or infamous, depending on who was describing it, brothel in town. Definitely in the wrong section of the city but elegant in its own overblown and gaudy way. It was well-known to every citizen, though the ladies never acknowledged its existence, and pretended those of their husbands who went there were merely *away on business* for the night.

Colin once remarked that quite a few citizens of Tipperary had late night business in that section of town. Padraig had been a very frequent visitor, when he wasn't cuckolding some husband or other. Donal went there many times while home from school, sneaking out after his parents were asleep so his mother wouldn't know, or saying he was going some place else, then heading there, though probably Quinton wouldn't have cared, since Colin had it for a fact his father had also done his own visiting in his wilder days before his marriage.

Once Donal married, his visits terminated abruptly, much to the madam's dismay, for Master Donal had been a big spender, not only for her girls' favors but also at the gaming tables on the first floor.

Colin's own visits had been few and far between, because he had a great deal of Padraig's reputation to overcome in Tipperary, but now that was over, also, thank God. Now he had no one's good name to worry about but his own.

Marriage seemed to be the one constant factor in ending visits to DeLancey's, at least in the McCoy family.

"Don, you're actually settin' foot inside here?" Colin asked as Phelan and Donal guided him up the steps.

"Merely to make certain you get home in one piece,"

his brother assured him.

"Phey, I thank you for this…" Colin turned to his friend, who gripped his elbow tightly as if fearing he'd run away.

"Think nothing of it."

"…but I'm afraid I'm goin' t' mimic me elder braithur here an' won't be partakin' o' any delights t'night."

"What?" Phelan released him so quickly they both nearly fell. "Man, this is your last night to have any woman you want, because I've a feeling you'll be carrying on that insane McCoy tradition an' won't be seeking other beds after your marriage." He shook a fist drunkenly. "Because if you do, I'll be coming after you myself. So why not…"

"Hold on, Phey," Colin said. "Maybe I'm a li'l touched in th' head by all this marriage business, but for some odd reason, I don't want anaithur woman, even now. I want no one but Fiona."

"You're certain?" Phelan looked unconvinced.

"I am."

"In that case, may I take your place as guest of honor and toss th four ladybirds I'd lined up for you?"

"Four? God, man, how virile do you think I am?"

"Enough for all of them or I wouldn't have asked."

"Be me guest." Colin made a drunken bow. "I'll perch mesel' in a chair at a card table an' guzzle some wine an' have a good enough time." He turned, looked at his brother, and nudged Donal in the ribs. "Eh, Donal?"

"Right, Col." His brother's answer sounded more patronizing than anything else.

Colin ignored that.

"Then let's go in. Look!" He nodded at the open doorway where a liveried footman waited, one who might've been mistaken for someone from a noble house except that his suit was of satin festooned with gold braid and sequins. "Everyone's already gone in. Come on!"

Colin staggered inside, dragging Donal and Phelan with him.

Their return home, at the much, much later hour of four o'clock in the morning, was noted by no one. Somehow, everyone staying at the Hall managed to get inside and to their own beds without waking anyone, either guests or servants. Colin needed a bit of help. He might not have indulged in women but he'd certain downed enough wine to make up for it as he lost at cards.

"Ah well…" He opined as he tossed the hand he held to the table. "Unlucky in cards, lucky in love…"

"I'm not certain that's the way it goes," Donal said. "But for you, I hope the gods make an exception."

"Shut up an' help me t' me horse," Colin ordered. At McCoy Hall, he paraphrased that, saying, "Shhh…help me get t' me room without fallin' o'er me big drunken feet."

"Want me to call Geoffrey?" Donal staggered as Colin's weight became almost a dead one, making his brother's knees abruptly buckle.

"Nay…don't wake th' lad…"

They stumbled inside. Donal guided Colin up the stairs and to his chambers, dumping him onto the bed. Colin fell face down and didn't move.

"Colin?" Donal punched his brother in the ribs. "Don't go to sleep. I've something I need to tell you, talk to you about, actually…something important…"

Colin didn't answer.

"Colin, damn it, no…wake up." Donal shook his shoulder. "Damn, why did I wait so long?"

Colin turned his head and snored softly.

"Colin!" Donal shook him.

Colin rolled away, burrowing his head into the pillow.

"This is important. I need to tell you…"

"Sir? Is everythin' all right?"

Geoffrey stood at the door. The valet was fully dressed and Donal imagined he'd been sitting in his room, listening for hoofbeats in the drive.

"No." He turned so quickly he nearly overbalanced. "He's…we've…merely celebrated a bit too much."

"I'll get him ready for bed." Geoffrey came over to the bed.

"No." Donal put a hand on his arm. "Pull off his boots and let him sleep as he is." He gave Colin an angry glare. "If he's stiff tomorrow from sleeping in his clothes, it's good enough."

He slapped Colin's shoulder. His brother didn't react.

"Col, you and I have to have a serious talk before your wedding."

With that, he stalked out.

Chapter 16

Colin was in the throes of the worst headache in existence.

After a scant two hours' sleep, he'd been rousted from bed by Geoffrey at the ungodly hour—at least, that's how he considered it—of six o'clock.

"Come, Master Colin. 'Tis time for you t' get up."

"Ohhh, nay, Geoffrey. What ails you, comin' in here so early an' disturbin' me slumbers?"

"Surely, you haven't forgotten what day it is, sir?" Geoffrey didn't remind Colin that he generally was up at least an hour earlier than this so he could make his *toilette* and have breakfast with the family around seven.

"What day is it?" Colin struggled to sit up, then collapsed onto his back on his pillow. When Geoffrey didn't answer, he lay there a moment before opening his eyes. "Nay, it can't be. So soon?"

"Aye, sir, 'tis your weddin' day, an' you've got t' get yourself out o' that bed an' start preparin' yourself."

With a groan, Colin heaved himself upright, shook his head, and threw back the covers, swinging his legs over the side of the bed.

"Why am I still in me clothes?"

"Because Master Donal said to leave you that way."

"Thank you, braithur," Colin said to the absent Donal. He looked concerned. "Geoffrey, I admit I remember very li'l o' last night after a certain point. We

144

didn't awaken anyone when we came in, did we? I'm assumin' me braithur was with me all th' way?"

"No, sir, you were both relatively quiet, and, yes, sir, Master Donal carried you up th' stairs himself."

"You know this for certain?"

"I was waitin' up, sir. I'm certain."

"Thank God for that, anyway. That we were quiet, I mean. I'd hate for me maithur t' have seen th' state I was in." He stood, tested his legs, and when they appeared able to hold him, took a step. "Well, now, me pins seem t' be workin' all right. Therefore...let's get busy. I've wasted enough time. Say, you didn't bring up any coffee, did you?"

"I did, sir." Geoffrey gestured to a small tray holding a coffee carafe and a cup he had set on the dressing table.

"Pour me a cup an' let's get started transformin' me inta a blushin' bridegroom, or whate'er 'tis called."

He hadn't eaten his usual hearty fare that morning, for abruptly as he sat down to table, his appetite, perhaps aided by the remnants of his previous night's drinking bout, turned traitor and fled. Colin brushed aside the coddled eggs, plate piled high with rashers of bacon and slabs of ham, the muffins and crumpets, and settled for several slices of well-buttered toast and two more cups of coffee. That at least didn't set his head a-jangling or his belly twisting.

Everyone had been conspicuously absent from breakfast, Donal included. Colin supposed his brother would be there and accompany him to the church, but the table was empty save for himself. When he questioned Cormac, the butler explained that Master Quinton had gone into town on some last-minute business...his mother and Mistress Felicity were changing into the gowns they would wear preparatory to traveling to Alisdaire Manor where they would ride in the wedding entourage to the church…and Master Donal had taken himself to the stables to select which carriage they would use.

Ignoring his headache, Colin drank his coffee, munched his toast, decided he was feeling better, and returned to his chambers. There, he deliberated on whether the suit Geoffrey had chosen was proper to be married in. With the valet's assistance, he dressed in the black morning coat and waistcoat, then dithered over whether the dove gray trousers or black ones would be more suitable. At last, he settled on black. Geoffrey wrapped, tied, and folded his cravat, produced his grandfather McCoy's gold watch and chain, with Fiona's heart-shaped fob attached, and draped it across his vest front from pocket-to-pocket, looping it over a center button of his vest.

With a bit more tweaking and a little further preening, they managed to kill another hour or so.

Then Colin began to pace.

There was to be no luncheon this day. The wedding dinner, held at Alisdaire Manor after the ceremony, was to take its place. Having digested his toast, Colin's belly protested that, then accepted with an occasional whine he hoped the thickness of his shirt, waistcoat, and coat would muffle.

Stopping in his third circuit of the hearth, Colin pondered whether to ride ahead to the church, then decided ten o'clock was too early to be there. What would he do, other than stand around and pace until it was time? He could do that as easily, and more comfortably, at home. He couldn't think of anything else to fill the time, however, though something niggled at the back of his memory…

"Geoffrey, did I imagine it, or did me braithur say last night…or this morning, rather…he had something he needed to discuss with me?"

"Yes, sir, I believe he did. He tried several times to rouse you enough to listen, but you were very deep in Morpheus' arms by that time."

"Hm. More like deep in Dionysus' arms, from all the wine I glugged down," Colin muttered. "Well, since he's not here, it must not have been too important."

He began to pace again, realized that was the third time he'd done so and stopped.

"I wonder what Fiona's doin' about now? I wish I could see her."

"Sir, you know 'tis bad luck t' see the bride afore th' ceremony."

"Aye, I know, but…who says 'tis bad luck? How do they know?"

"Do you want t' test th' theory, sir?"

"Nay. I've a feeling thin's are going t' be serious enough without me addin' t' them by challengin' that ol' sayin'." He shrugged the matter away and sat on the edge of a nearby chair. "Help me off with me boots, Geoff."

"Sir?"

"Me boots. I want them off." Colin raised a leg, thrusting it out stiffly.

Silently, the valet caught the heel and instep and pulled off the ankle-length Wellington. The other was removed as quickly and both set carefully in front of the wardrobe. Geoffrey had spent the good part of an hour the evening before polishing them with a fresh biscuit and egg white and didn't want anything to mar their gloss.

Colin got to his feet and removed his coat.

"Take this, also."

"Sir, why are you…"

Colin threw himself into the center of the bed one of the housemaids had tidied while he was eating his toast.

"I'm goin' t' take a nap," he announced, settling himself on his back. "Goin' t' stop pacin' an' conserve me energy for t'night. At least, I hope I'll need it t'night."

At Geoffrey's smirk, he went on, "Is that a leer I see? Not showin' me th' proper respect, are you? Or are you darin' t' think of what me bride an' I'll be doin'?"

"I'm afraid I'm not givin' you th' proper respect, sir," Geoffrey agreed. "As for your bride…I fear all I have for Miss Fiona is sympathy. At the moment, you remind me o' a child impatient for Father Christmas t' arrive."

"The gift I'll be given t'night isn't somethin' that old gentleman usually brings," Colin retorted. "What am I doin' discussin' me weddin' night with you? Get on with you an' your scandalous thoughts afore I box your ears!"

He waved a hand dramatically and turned his attention to the bed.

"With a li'l luck, I won't do much movin' around in me sleep an' muss me clothes. I certainly don't wear me boots to bed, hence…they're off, an' so is me jacket." He settled his arms across his midriff. "Wake me around twelve-thirty. Then I'll be ready t' go t' th' church."

****

Colin was in the vestry to the left of the altar. With Geoffrey following, he'd been escorted there by an acolyte whom he recognized as one of the lads from a nearby village. The boy left, the valet also deserting him.

"I can't stay, sir, but Master Donal should be along soon."

Thus, Colin waited...and got more anxious...and hungrier. It was nearing one o'clock and the breakfast he'd eaten had disappeared completely. He was certain he heard a discreet growl or two from his innards. He'd seen no one and heard nothing since the door shut behind Geoffrey. Now, he was almost in a panic.

Something had happened. Fiona had decided she didn't want him and eloped with Phelan Foyle...his mother had fallen down the stairs and they were searching frantically to take him to her bedside and no one remembered where he might be...a thousand and one disasters rushed through Colin's mind and out again as he told himself he was being fanciful and...oh, how he wished he had a goblet of wine to banish the remnants of his headache!

The door opened. Donal came in.

"Well! Good mornin', braithur...or is it afternoon yet?" Colin greeted him sarcastically. "Did I hear th' church bell tollin' just now, announcin' someone's nuptials t'day, perhaps...or more like a funeral?"

"I see you've recovered from last night." Donal ignored his brusque speech. "Good, for I've some things to say that you weren't in any condition to hear then."

"Ne'er mind that." Colin brushed aside whatever his brother wanted to say. "Is e'erythin' going well? Is the weddin' still on?"

"Of course, it is, dunce," Donal exclaimed. "Why shouldn't it be?"

"How should I know? I've been sequestered in here for hours. I thought perhaps some disaster had o'ertaken th' town. For all I knew, I was th' last man alive..."

"If that were so, you'd have more to worry about than a mere wedding," Donal muttered.

"Is there any wine in here?" Colin asked, looking around. "Where do they keep that for th' Sacrament?"

"Certainly not in here and you couldn't drink that if they did," Donal snapped. "Colin, we don't have much time and there's something I have to say."

Colin turned away, opening a small cupboard and peering inside.

"Colin! Stop moving around and look at me."

"Whate'er 'tis, can't it wait?"

"No, it can't. I tried to tell you last night, but you... You have to know this before the wedding."

"If 'tis about what's t' happen on me weddin' night, I'm no ignorant virgin. You saw t' that yourself, remember?" Colin reminded him. "I've a bit o' me own technique now, so I don't need any instruction."

"It's not that. It's... Will you please sit down?"

"All right, Donal." At last, his brother's agitation got through. Colin dropped into a chair, hands clasped at his knees. "What is it?"

"Colin...I...God, this is going to sound so coldblooded...you have to get Fiona with child as soon as possible."

"You're right. That is coldblooded, an' none o' your damned business when I do such a thin'." Colin's headache disappeared in the surprise of his brother's words. "Anyway, I'd thought t' delay that part o' marriage for a bit. Get accustom t' bein' a husband an' enjoy that a while before makin' meself into a faithur. I still use a lambskin like you told me, an' I've got that *interruptus* business perfected t' th' minute." Colin realized he was saying too much and snapped defensively, "What's it t' you, anyway?"

Donal bit his lip, swallowed loudly, and said, "Faithur wants a grandchild. To carry on the McCoy name…"

"I know. An' you'll give him one. Some day."

"No. I won't."

"What do you mean? Of course…"

"I can't sire children, Col." Don averted his face as if he couldn't look at his brother and make this admission. He flushed. "I'm sterile."

"Oh, now, that's a lie…" Colin blurted before he realized it. "What about that bastard Da's been payin' for all these years?"

Donal stared at him. "How do you know about that?"

"I heard you two talkin'. Th' night o' th' ball," Colin confessed. "Th' study door wasn't shut." He shrugged. "I eavesdropped."

"I *knew* I heard you pause on the stairs." Donal declared. He looked angry. "That was underhanded o' you."

"So is your lyin' like that. Why would you say such a thin', Don?"

"All right…" Donal didn't argue. "I'm going to tell you something and you have to swear you'll never speak it to another living soul."

"'Tis that bad?"

Donal nodded.

"All right, then. I swear." Colin held up a hand. "Now, what's this all about?"

"It's Felicity…she's the one who…she's barren…"

"Ah, nay…" Colin breathed his shock.

"It was some childhood accident, while she was

riding. The doctor told her parents she recovered, but later, after we were married and she didn't quicken…" Donal heaved a heart-heavy sigh. "Another examination proved something went wrong. We'll never have a child."

"Is that why you didn't go t' her while you were visitin'?"

"I suppose you heard what I told Father. That was the truth."

"Are you going t' divorce her?"

"Of course not. I love her, Col."

"I know you said that, but I thought…"

"I meant it, and I don't want her ever shamed by someone knowing she's the cause of our childlessness." Donal looked angry.

"An' what about your byblow?"

"The child died, along with his mother. Eight years ago. I…" Donal stopped, shaking his head. "You think I'm cold, but I swear…"

Colin shook his head. If anything, he thought his brother was feeling more than he was showing.

"We talked about it, Felicity and I… We were going to adopt the child, raise him as he should've been raised, as a McCoy."

"He?"

"I had a son, Colin." Donal sniffed, abruptly and loudly. "For two years, I had a son and didn't know it, and now…all I have is a rubbing of his headstone." He made a helpless, vague gesture. "Quinton Donal Nordin, that was his name." He looked away. "Didn't mean to make this confession time. I didn't intend to bring such sorry news and put a pall on your wedding day."

"I'm sorry, Donal." Colin wasn't certain whether he

was commiserating with his brother because of what he'd revealed or because he would now silently mourn that unknown child. *I had a nephew.*

"Thank you, Col, but at least I have Felicity." His brother's green eyes met Colin's, his gaze seeming to bore into them. "I truly love her." He sighed. "That's the 'for better or for worse' part. I love her no matter what."

There was a knock on the door. At Colin's call, another altar boy, resplendent in red cassock and white surplice, peeked in. "The reverend sent me t' tell you th' guests are here an' 'tis time for th' ceremony."

"We'll be right out." Donal told him.

The boy nodded and shut the door.

"Now you know." Donal spoke hurriedly. "Promise me you won't mention this to anyone, and please…do what you must. I'm counting on you, Col."

"As if I don't have enough t' worry me t'day," Colin muttered. He put a hand on his brother's shoulder. "Don't worry, Donal. Th' McCoy name'll go on for anaithur generation, at least, if I have anything t' do with it. Now then, shall we get me married so I can begin me labors?"

He shook his head in mock disgust.

"Ah, 'tis a terrible chore you've set me, braithur."

Colin's thoughts were awhirl as he stood beside Donal at the altar. What his brother told him was astounding, shocking, and enough to make him want to go searching for a good stiff drink. *What if 'twere Fiona an' me? Do I love her enough t' grow old with her in a barren marriage…childless…just th' two o' us?*

He was startled by the sudden admiration he felt for his brother, mingled with an overwhelming pity. Loving a woman so much he'd willingly give up any chance of having a child of his own. Opening himself to the ridicule, mostly whispered behind fingers, of sterility to protect his wife from the same scorn, of having his manhood questioned most cruelly.

Colin raised his head, forcing his thoughts onto more soothing planes.

He had a brief glimpse of the silver tray placed on the altar with the Host and chalice, covered by a crimson cloth, was aware of the scent of incense mingling with the sharp, tang of fresh-cut greenery and the spicy but mellow scent of roses and myrtle. He forced himself to look out over the congregation, gilded in the golden glow of candles and the sun's multicolored hues as it filtered through the stained glass windows.

On the left side, in the first pew, sat his mother and father. Màiri was gorgeous in a teal-blue gown trimmed with bruxelles lace of the same color. One of those ridiculous little pancake-shaped bonnets perched atop her graying curls. She was clutching an already sodden handkerchief.

Why is she crying, anyway?

Seated beside her was Colin's sister Bridget and her husband and the eldest of their children, Eamon, now ten and declared old enough this year to attend something as serious as a wedding and being able to behave. At the moment, however, Bridget was leaning over, speaking to him and her expression said she wondered if she'd been wrong in her assessment of her son's maturity.

In the second row was Màiri's sister and her sister's husband, and his father's widowed sister, dressed in dark lavender acceptable for widowhood yet also festive enough for a wedding. Next to her sat Quinton's uncle Seamus and his cousin Connell, their Black Irish looks out of place among the red-haired crowd. That pew also held the cousins not participating in the wedding.

Across the aisle, Lady Alisdaire and the Alisdaire relatives occupied corresponding benches. Her Ladyship was regally begowned in delicate rose and pink, and was holding a handkerchief as tear-soaked as Màiri's.

Behind them sat the guests. Colin was surprised to see how full the church was. *When did I get so many relatives?* His side of the church was as filled as Fiona's side, if not more so.

The candles flickered as someone opened the door to the church. From outside, the sound of horses' stamping and snorting floated in. There were footsteps entering the narthex, the jingle of bits as the carriages drove away.

His thoughts were interrupted by the changing of the organ music into a stately and solemn processional of some kind. Figures appeared in the doorway of the narthex, a single young woman, Fiona's maid of honor, then three young men, each escorting a young lady. They entered the nave, coming down the aisle, parting as they approached the chancel. The young men, in this case, two McCoy cousins and Phelan Foyle, stopped beside Colin and Donal, the young women, three of Fiona's friends, going to the left and standing next to the maid of honor before the first pew.

There was an abrupt and startling silence. The organist struck a chord harsh in its loudness. Everyone stood, looking toward the back of the church.

Fiona and Lord Alisdaire appeared.

Colin took a deep breath and thought he might stifle. She was beautiful.

Donal placed a hand on his shoulder. Colin didn't

glance at him. He inhaled loudly and Donal's hand fell away.

Compared to that of her attendants, Fiona's wedding dress was simple, but its sheer simplicity made it elegant. It was fashioned of cream silk with a billowy overskirt draped with lace and tulle. Colin remembered Fiona telling him she had wanted a train but had been talked out of that feature because Lady Alisdaire reminded her she didn't have any cousins young enough to be train bearers. On her head she wore pearls and white satin ribbon woven into a fillet, to which her veil was attached.

Fiona wore no jewelry except the pearl-and-diamond brooch Colin had given her at the dinner the night before, and earrings which had been her grandmother's. She carried a bouquet of two white roses and sprigs of lilies of the valley.

During the walk down the aisle, she kept her gaze demurely downcast. As they neared where Colin stood, she looked up, saw him, and smiled. Colin took a step toward her. All thoughts left his mind except those concerning the young woman before him.

I'd do anythin' for you. I love you more than Donal loves Felicity, I swear.

Lord Alisdaire paused, slid Fiona's hand from his arm, and took a step back. Without waiting for him to take Colin's hand, she reached over and clasped it in hers. Colin transferred her hand to his own arm, and His Lordship dropped into the pew next to his wife.

Abruptly, she stumbled. Colin paused, startled to see Fiona's lips trembling. She pulled her hand from his, raising it to her mouth.

"Steady, lass," he whispered. "Only a bit more t' go an' 'tis o'er."

That made her smile. She slid her hand back into the crook of his elbow. Colin led her the last few steps to the altar where Reverend Hennessey stood.

The wedding party turned to face the altar. Donal took a step closer, hand automatically going to the pocket in his jacket where he'd placed the ring. Behind them in the first row of family pews, there were twin muffled sobs from Màiri and Lady Alisdaire and equal movements from Quinton and His Lordship as they laid comforting hands on their wives' arms.

Clearing his throat, the reverend opened his prayer book…

Chapter 17

"To the good health of Mr. and Mrs. Colin McCoy."
Phelan made the toast without a quaver.

"Hear, hear." Donal raised his glass as did the others.

"T' you, me beautiful lass." Colin's whisper was for Fiona alone to hear.

She blushed and sipped her wine.

After that came speeches and more speeches, more than had been said at the pre-wedding banquet. All Colin could do was wonder how anyone had any more good wishes for them, since he'd have sworn all had been said at the previous supper. He listened, smiling, certain his expression was becoming obviously fixed, while his body stifled his desire to fidget with impatience.

Get finished, why don't they? So's we can leave without bein' rude.

He was fast approaching not really caring how rude it appeared. He wanted to be out of there and at the hunting lodge with no one around for miles, except him and his wife. Even if they wouldn't really be alone, with Geoffrey and Edith, and a coachman and footman with them, housed in the servants' cottage.

Damn, why does everythin' have t' be so complicated an' proper? E'en a weddin' night? Briefly, he wondered what Padraig's wedding in that far-off Nebraska had been like.

Eventually the toasts dwindled to a halt and supper was served and enjoyed, though later Colin would swear he hadn't tasted a thing. Afterward, he didn't even remember what was served. Fiona also appeared to have no appetite. She simply rearranged the food on her plate.

Is she thinkin' o' later? He hoped she wasn't dreading it.

The banquet finished, they adjourned to the ballroom where the bride and groom had their first waltz together. Colin relished holding Fiona close, feeling the satin and silk crinkle as it was crushed against his waistcoat, enjoying the sound of fabric swishing as her skirts swirled and brushed against his trouser legs.

Others joined them on the floor. He thought Donal looked remarkably debonair as he spun Felicity around. His wife appeared more fragile and doll-like than ever beside his tall figure. He felt a twinge of...*something*...as he caught Donal's eye and his brother looked quickly away. Donal seemed preoccupied. Perhaps thinking of his own wedding day and how so much unexpected had followed?

Quinton whirled Màiri past. His mother was smiling. She always liked to dance. Lord Alisdaire was being remarkably agile for someone his age and his wife was smiling at him.

Colin pulled Fiona even closer, brushing a fairly discreet kiss across her lips. She went abruptly lax against him.

"Lass?" Hoping not to attract attention, he escorted her from the floor to a nearby divan. "Are you all right?" He bent to whisper.

"I'm fine, Colin." Her voice sounded hearty enough. "I'm merely tired of all this folderol. Why can't we leave?" She clasped his hand, looking up at him. "I wish to be alone with you…husband."

Husband. That word sent a chill of surprise as well as a tremor of expectancy down his spine. She was as impatient as he.

"Colin?" A hand on his shoulder turned him away from his bride. Donal pulled him a few feet from the divan. "A word?"

"What is it?" Colin snapped. He glanced back at Fiona who was watching him and her new brother-in-law.

Someone else came up to the divan. Felicity. She bent to speak to Fiona, who reluctantly looked away to answer.

"Not now, Donal." The last thing Colin wanted was to speak to his brother. "I think we said all there was t' say this mornin'."

"We did, but this isn't about that," Donal interrupted, looking past him. He nodded to someone.

Colin glanced back, seeing Felicity return the nod. Donal shook his arm, making Colin look back at him.

"All I want to say is I wish the best for you, little brother."

"Thanks for that." Colin's answer was short. "When can we leave? I suppose I'm eager t' get t' carryin' out my part o' extendin' th' McCoy name…an' all that goes inta doin' that."

"Generally, the bride and groom have to stay until at least half the evening is over." Donal ignored the last part of his statement.

"Ah, nay." Colin envisioned himself falling asleep on one of the divans.

"But I see no reason why you have to follow all that

dreary old custom," Donal continued. "Felicity and I did and it was sore vexing, I remember." He laughed softly. "I was ready to leap onto the table, knock away the dishes, throw her upon it, and have my way then and there."

"Really?" That made Colin stare at his brother. "You could've fooled me. I was there, remember? I thought you were the most fantastically controlled groom I'd ever seen."

"Exactly how many grooms had you seen at that age?" Donal tugged on his arm. "Look, Col, I'm sure you'd prefer Padraig were here for this, but I'm afraid I'll have to do."

Briefly, there was a spark of the old pre-university Donal in his eyes.

"Come on." He backed away. "Act natural, don't attract attention."

"Where are we goin'?" Colin asked.

"To escape."

"That's more like it!" Colin gave him brother a grin.

Carefully, they strolled a few paces, then paused and after a moment, backed toward a door to the side of the ballroom. No one appeared to be paying the two any attention. Colin glanced back at the divan. It was empty.

"Where's Fiona?"

"Changing, no doubt." Donal pulled Colin through the door.

Once they were in the little hallway leading to the kitchen, the sounds of voices and music died away. Donal hurried Colin along.

"Don't I need t' change, too?"

"To what?" Donal asked. "You look ready for travel, but Fiona couldn't possibly get into the coach with all those crinolines and ruffles."

Colin conceded that was true enough. Hadn't he thought the same thing that day they drove to the lake?

They arrived in the kitchen where the cook and her helpers were washing dishes and cleaning up. The scully, up to her elbows in soapy water, saw them and stopped, lifting her hands to dip them a damp curtsey and leaving wet prints on her skirts. The others followed suit and Colin managed a hasty bow as Donal rushed him through and out the tradesman's entrance. Behind him, the scully turned back to her chore and several giggles followed him through the door.

"They're laughin'," he accused. "At me."

"Envy." Donal dismissed servant talk. "For Fiona."

Colin didn't answer.

At the rear of the house, the coach waited, with a footman standing beside the door. Colin and Fiona's luggage was lashed on top, everything they might need on their wedding trip. Three figures were visible inside. Felicity stood beside the coach, clutching her cashmere shawl about her shoulders.

"How did Fiona get here so fast?"

"Felicity helped her. I imagine that was the fastest that lass has ever been gotten out of her clothes." Donal allowed himself a smidge of a leer. "Until you're alone with her tonight."

"Sir." Colin pulled away with a good imitation of insult. "You're speakin' o' me wife."

"Just don't forget that, brother…and always be sensitive to her needs."

The footman opened the coach door,

"Now, get in there." Donal shoved Colin inside.

He staggered in, falling onto the seat. The footman

slammed the door. There was the sound of him scrambling onto his place at the back of the coach. Felicity stepped to Donal's side. They raised their hands in farewell. The coachman snapped the whip and the horses started off.

Inside, it was so dim, Colin could barely make out his fellow travelers' faces. With a bit of anger, he discovered he was sitting beside Geoffrey, with Edith and Fiona opposite.

What th' hell? Isn't it proper for a man t' sit beside his wife? His father always sat by his mother and Donal sat with Felicity. *I can understand why it might not be before, but now...*

Briefly, he was tempted to seize Geoff and physically exchange him for Fiona. *Wouldn't that be a to-do? Nay, Geoff weighs as much as I. I probably couldn't e'en lift him.*

The little maid was stiff-backed and silent, as was his wife. Fiona was wearing some sort of traveling suit that Colin imagined he'd appreciate if it were daylight so he could see it. As it was, she looked as if she were wrapped in a bulky, dark garment that could've been anything from a blanket to an opera cape.

Fiona leaned forward, caught his hands, and squeezed them tightly. He thought her fingers trembled. Unmindful of valet or maid, Colin raised them and kissed the backs of her hands.

Briefly, her fingers caressed his lips. Then she pulled away and leaned back, hands placidly in her lap.

"Well, glad t' be away from all that din." Colin attempted conversation. "I appreciated th' best wishes, but it was beginnin' t' become tiresome."

There was a long silence.

"Yes. I agree." Fiona's response was a timid whisper.

After that, no one spoke until they reached the lodge.

Chapter 18

Their journey took several hours. Colin tried more conversation, but after a few monosyllables from Fiona and a couple of asides from Geoff, with absolutely no response from Edith, he gave up. He attempted to entertain himself by watching the passing scenery, but it was now so dark all he could see were shapeless blobs he knew were reasonably trees and houses but looked more like bogies from one of his childhood nightmares.

Gradually, the houses disappeared and there was nothing but forest on either side. Once they went over a bridge, the horses' hooves clattering, then stamping again on hard-pounded dirt.

The monotonous sound and the swaying of the coach had a sonorous effect. Several times, Colin caught his eyelids drooping and once actually jerked himself upright as his head toppled forward into near-sleep. Geoffrey hadn't spoken, but a quick glance at the valet revealed he was wide awake.

How does he do it? Colin was aware Geoffrey had been up hours before he, and while he was enduring that wedding banquet and dance ordeal, was busy packing his bags and making certain they were loaded onto the coach. *Surely he's tired also. It certainly doesn't show. Perhaps valets have some inner resilience th' rest o' us mere mortals don't.*

Across from him, Fiona was enveloped in shadows,

so silent Colin wondered if she'd fallen victim to the coach's rocking and actually dozed. Little Edith had definitely succumbed. The maid was slouched sideways, her head resting on her mistress' shoulder. Occasionally a snore like a kitten's mew issued from her lax lips.

"Here we are, sir." Geoffrey spoke, leaning toward the window and glancing out. He removed his watch from his waistcoat pocket, squinting at it. "Made good time, too."

As the coach pulled up in front of the lodge and halted, the lack of movement brought everyone to attentiveness, except Edith.

"Edith?" Gently, Fiona shook her. "Wake up, dear. We're here."

"Uh…wha…" The girl started slightly, sat up and looked around. "I-I wasn't asleep, Miss. I was merely restin' me eyes."

"Of course," Fiona answered, patting her shoulder. "We're here anyway."

The footman jumped down and opened the door. Colin nearly fell out, regaining his balance and offering Fiona his hand. She emerged a little more elegantly. He turned to the lodge as Geoffrey followed, assisting Edith.

"The servants' cabin is in back," Colin told the coachman. "As is th' stable. Bed down th' horses an' go ahead an' retire. Geoffrey an' th' maid will be along shortly."

It was going to be very shortly indeed, if he had anything to say about it.

The driver nodded, shook the reins, and the coach rumbled away.

The lanterns hanging at each side of the lodge door were lit, illuminating the long veranda and porch railings. The shutters were open and light shone through the windows. Quinton had sent servants ahead earlier in the day to open the lodge and make certain linens in the master bedroom were changed and fresh, as well as food being in the larder for breakfast. They were ordered to make certain all the lamps were filled and left lit.

The lodge had been in the McCoy family for generations. Colin's great-great-grandfather entertained his friends there during hunting parties, bringing back game to be cooked at a banquet the following night. Colin's grandfather as well as Quinton had celebrated their own wedding nights in the lodge. In an indiscreet moment, Quinton bragged to his sons that Donal had been conceived in the bed in the master bedchamber during a weekend he and Màiri stole away to be by themselves.

The family itself had spent many happy days there, where the children could play among the trees, skip stones across the little brook running nearby, wade in its waters, and try to catch tadpoles. When Quinton became Lord Alisdaire's steward, he invited His Lordship and his wife for that quiet family gathering during which Samuel caught the frog sending Fiona into tears.

Until now, that was the only time someone from His Lordship's family had set foot in the lodge.

The building was made entirely of logs from the forest, roughhewn and unplaned, to give it a further rustic air. Unlike a gamekeepers' cabin or the lodge employed by the villagers given permission to hunt on McCoy land, it was built on a very grand and much larger scale. With a parlor, dining room, a games room with a billiard table, and a kitchen, the fact it had only fourteen bedrooms upstairs made it a *small* lodge compared to some.

Geoffrey pushed past, going up the steps. He was carrying a small portmanteau filled with whatever Colin needed for his morning *toilette*. Setting down the case, he pulled a key from his pocket. It had been entrusted to him by Quinton earlier that day. Opening the door, he stepped aside, taking one of the lanterns from its hook and holding it high.

Colin and Fiona came up the steps. At the threshold, Colin stopped, peering inside. What he could see was as it always had been when he came with his father and some of Quinton's friends to hunt. Somehow, he'd expected to find it changed, a new and forbidding place, as if he were a stranger barging in and taking possession of someone else's property.

He hesitated.

"Colin?"

That one word brought him out of whatever held him. Without a word, he released Fiona's hand and swung her into his arms, stepping across the threshold and into the lodge. He took several steps bringing him to the center of the little foyer and stopped, swinging her in a circle.

Fiona laughed. He kissed her. Her arms went around his neck and she returned the kiss before they broke away as Geoffrey came inside with Edith. The little maid was carrying Fiona's case with another, smaller one for herself under her arm.

"Colin, it's lovely." Fiona looked around. Half the fuel lamps set in wall sconces burned, lighting the downstairs. Light from a single wall lamp on the landing trickled down the stairs, leaving the upper story in half-shadow.

"Wait until you see th' bedchamber," he whispered and winked.

Though she blushed slightly, he thought her expression was remarkably eager.

Setting Fiona on her feet, he affected a brisk attitude. "Ahem…I imagine you're a bit fashed, me dear, as am I." He glanced at Geoffrey, gaze darting away as he saw the valet's bright expression, and looked at Edith instead. "Edith, help your mistress prepare for bed. 'Tis th' first door on th' right up th' stairs."

Face reflecting Fiona's own blush, Edith bobbed a curtsey and practically ran for the stairs, only to be nearly jerked off her feet as Geoffrey caught her arm. He handed her the lantern.

"In case th' room isn't lit."

She fumbled a moment, changing hands so the case was in her left, and nearly dropping the one under her arm. She took the lantern, looked at Fiona and said, "Miss?"

Silently, Fiona went with her.

Colin watched them go up the stairs into the dimness. The lantern made a soft glowing spot in the darkness of the stairs, throwing their shadows over him and Geoffrey. Behind him, he heard the valet take one of the wall lanterns from its niche. He waited until he heard a door open and close, then slapped the valet on the arm.

"Come on, Geoff. How fast can you get me out o' these clothes an' ready for me bride?"

"I can do the former in th' blink o' an eye, sir," Geoffrey's voice held laughter. "As for th' latter, do you really need any help for that?" He looked down.

Colin followed his gaze. Leave it to good old Geoff to say the obvious. He was partially aroused but hadn't even realized it. He hoped neither Fiona nor Edith had noticed.

"Quite so." *Oh damn, that sounded so much like Donal in his stiff-necked Britisher mode.* He started up the stairs.

They went into the first bedroom on the left. Geoffrey set the lantern on a nearby table and proceeded to place the portmanteau on the bed. Unsnapping the locks, he flipped it open and stared at the contents.

In the meantime, Colin shucked his coat, tossing it onto a nearby chair.

"Sir? What's this?"

He turned to see Geoffrey lift a garment from the case, holding it by the shoulders as he shook it open. Colin's dressing gown, a deep blue velvet creation, already lay on the bed.

"What does it look like?" There was a bit of irritation in his voice.

"It looks like a gentleman's nightshirt, but surely you're not wearin' that t'night?"

"I'm tryin' t' be aware o' me new wife's sensibilities," Colin snapped, wondering at the same time why he had to justify his actions to his valet, especially tonight. "I don't want t' shock her by exposin' her t' th' full force o' me masculinity all at once."

"I...see..." Geoffrey didn't add any facetious comment as he expected, but simply laid the garment on the bed and stepped toward him.

He began to unwrap Colin's cravat, untying and unwinding the length of linen until it was free of his master's neck. He laid it in the chair also while Colin waited impatiently. It took only another moment to unbutton his cuffs and pull the shirt over his head.

170

Colin dropped into another chair and Geoffrey divested him of his boots, placing them under the chair holding his clothing.

"If you can handle your trousers, sir," the valet said as he straightened. "I think a spit bath is in order. 'Tis been a most tense day for you, I imagine, an' you need a bit o' a wash t' remove some o' th' nervous sweat you've accumulated."

"How did you get so perceptive?" Colin stood and began to unbutton the side panels of his trousers.

"That's part o' a valet's job description, sir...thinkin' ahead." Geoffrey went to a nearby dressing table where an ironstone pitcher and basin sat. He peered into the pitcher. "Hmm, water looks fresh. Perhaps they filled the pitcher when they opened th' lodge earlier."

He lifted it and poured.

"How did you learn all this stuff, anyway?" Colin asked, more for something to fill the silence than because he wanted to know. Talking was better than whistling in the dark. "Do they teach it at valet school?"

"There *are* such places, sir," Geoffrey replied. "However, me father taught me what he knew, an' I learned the rest by watchin' an' listenin' an'...." He picked up a small towel and draped it over his arm, then dropped a washcloth into the basin. "...from observin' you."

"Me?" Colin stepped out of the trousers and added them to the chair, then untied the waistband of his smallclothes and removed them also. He shivered slightly, then wondered why. It wasn't cold, and he'd been naked before Geoffrey at least once a day because the valet always helped him dress and undress. Perhaps since this was such a momentous occasion Geoffrey was

171

helping him prepare for?

"Yes, sir." Geoffrey brought basin and washcloth to a lamp table and set it down. He lifted the washcloth, wringing it. "You have certain ways you like things done. Quite a lot o' them…an' I have t' remember all."

He took a step toward Colin and rubbed the cloth across his face in a brisk, no-nonsense manner, over his ears, down his neck.

Colin grimaced, thinking this was almost like being a child in the nursery again, with a nanny making certain he was clean and presentable. Geoffrey had done this many times, but for some reason, tonight, it felt odd. The wet cloth traveled across his chest and ribs, making a detour to delve slightly into his navel.

Geoffrey knelt to wipe his thighs and calves and lift one foot, swathing it briefly with the wet cloth. Colin clutched the bedpost to keep his balance as he steadied himself.

The other foot was subsequently wiped and the valet continued behind him, bringing the cloth up over his buttocks and back and across his shoulders.

"There."

Geoffrey returned to the basin, leaving Colin with flesh damp and even more shivery. Goosebumps abruptly prickled his skin.

The valet soaked the cloth and wrung it, and turned back, sliding a hand under Colin's ghoolies and wick, carefully brushing the damp cloth down his shaft and around his balls.

"Better give those a second swipe," Colin ordered. "…considerin'."

Geoffrey obeyed but didn't answer. Apparently, he also knew when to be discreet about a delicate subject, or perhaps he was abruptly sympathetic with Colin's own eagerness. Colin had a sudden curiosity about his valet's intimate life and realized he had absolutely no idea what Geoffrey did on his free days.

Dropping the cloth back into the basin, Geoffrey picked up the towel and gave Colin's still-damp body an abrupt and brisk rubdown.

"Now that's out o' th' way…" Colin glanced at the nightshirt.

Geoffrey walked over to the bed, but instead of picking up the shirt, he reached into the case and brought out a small vial. Opening it, he tilted the little glass bottle and poured a bit of its contents onto his palms. Rubbing his hands together, he returned to where Colin stood.

"Is that…" Colin took a deep breath. "Sandalwood?"

"Yes, sir."

"I don't know, Geoff, do you think I need…"

Colin rarely indulged in applying sandalwood, especially after he'd learned it was considered an aphrodisiac. He'd worn it once to the Church and the girl he'd chosen seemed to go wild. That bout had been so physically exhausting for him he'd sworn never to wear it again…and now, here was his valet preparing to anoint him with the stuff?

"I don't think so."

"I'm only usin' one drop, sir." Geoffrey held up his hands, letting Colin see the glistening smear on his palms. "Only a bit, t' ease the way, so t' speak." He touched Colin's face, brushing across his cheeks and down each side of his neck, then stepped back.

"I suppose that's…"

Geoffrey bent and swiped both hands against

Colin's groin.

"Geoff! What th' hell?"

"Just ridding myself o' th' excess, sir. It can't hurt." Geoffrey's answer was so matter-of-fact Colin was shocked.

"Perhaps not," Colin reluctantly agreed.

I certainly don't need any help t' make love to me wife, but perhaps it might assist me in doin' what's required as far as th' family's concerned. Though he was of the opinion he didn't need any help doing *anything* required of him.

Geoffrey held up the nightshirt. It was simple in its design, and that alone hinted at its expensiveness. Fashioned of white cotton, round-necked, with a smocked and divided yoke buttoned down the chest, it fell to a few inches below the knee, with that usual opening at the bottom.

A little too delicately sewn, for a *real* man's tastes, Colin decided, but since he hoped not to wear it long, he decided he could briefly tolerate the ruffles on the cuffs and the white silk embroidery on the collar.

"I commend you on your concern, sir." Geoffrey dropped the shirt over Colin's head and smoothed it down his hips. "If you wish t' be very careful o' your wife's sensibilities tonight, an' want t'…uh…ease…inta bein' a husband, you can always use th' Glory Hole."

"Eh?" Colin gave him a stare, wondering if the valet was being vulgar somehow. He'd never heard that phrase before. "Glory Hole? What's that?"

"Why this, sir." Geoffrey touched the appliqué sewn into the center of the shirt at thigh-length, that open place Colin had always wondered about. "Surely you know…"

"That thing's been on all me nightshirts, but…"

"You never thought t' ask what it was for, sir?" Geoff sounded surprised.

Colin didn't know why he should. Hadn't the valet helped him into his sleepwear since he was sixteen? Had he ever heard a comment about that bit of stitchery?

"Wasn't that curious." Studying the appliqué, Colin caught up the nightshirt, rubbing his thumb over the stitching around the Glory Hole. "I always thought 'twas t' piss through." He ran his fingers along the plaquette. "You mean that's for… Well, now…"

He wondered how the seamstress had felt as she sewed it into place.

"So, you've never used one, sir?"

He felt the valet was pushing the subject a bit.

"As far as I'm concerned, 'tis a *useless thin'.*" *Unnecessary, too.* "When I'm in bed with a doxy, I'm always naked, anyway, an' quite frankly, th' idea o' insertin' me member through a slit in a shirt so I can thrust it into a warm female body is absurd." Colin surprised himself by the heat with which he spoke.

He wanted nothing between him and his goal, especially not a stiff and starched length of cotton.

He continued fiddling with the plaquette as Geoffrey reminded, "But tonight, you're not with a doxy, sir. This is Miss Fiona, an'…"

Colin's finger went inside the plaquette. "Here, now, Geoff…th' damned thing's sewn shut! What good is that?"

"Oh? Shouldn't be." Geoff knelt, thrusting his own fingers inside the fold of cloth. Sure enough, it was stitched tightly. "Doubtless th' seamstress forgot t' clip it. That's no problem, sir."

He reached into a pocket, bringing out a penknife

and flicking it open.

"Just a few snips an' it'll be in workin' order." He held up the knife. "If you want it open, that is?"

"Just do it," Colin snapped. All this folderol about a bit of thread and cloth was wasting time.

Several minutes later, the Glory Hole was open and a small pile of cut threads lay on the bedroom floor. Geoffrey snapped closed the knife. Scooping up the threads, he put them and the knife into his pocket, and got to his feet.

"There, sir, ready…for…whatever." He pulled Colin's dressing gown from the bed and held it while his master thrust his arms into the sleeves. As Colin buttoned the front, he picked up the lantern. "Are you ready, sir?"

Colin fiddled with the Glory Hole, images flittering through his mind he wasn't going to share with anyone. He buttoned the dressing gown, saw his slippers by the bed and stepped into them.

"As I'll e'er be."

Geoffrey stepped to the door, opened it, and bowed. Colin walked through. He strode across the landing to the master bedroom. From under the door, he saw light shining, but there was no sound. Raising his fist, he knocked.

The door opened to reveal Edith standing there. She hurried out so fast he hadn't a chance to see past her as she shut the door behind her. In her hand she held one of the little cases she'd carried into the bedchamber. She looked up at him.

"Which room should I take, sir?"

"You'll be sleepin' in th' servants' cabin…" Colin began.

"Oh, sir." she looked absolutely shocked. "I

couldn't."

"I'm afraid that'd be most improper, sir," Geoffrey put in smoothly. "A lone servin' maid sleepin' in a cabin with four menservants?" His tone implied Colin should've known this.

"I guess not." Colin was dismayed. Why hadn't he thought of that? Why hadn't he even realized it? Because he never bothered to be concerned with the proprieties where servants were concerned. "So where…?"

He looked around.

"Edith can have that one." Geoffrey nodded to a door at the end of the hall, as far from the master bedchamber as could be. He opened it and ushered the girl inside. Colin wondered if this was another thing Geoffrey had observed…and when had he suddenly taken charge, anyway?

The maid trotted in furtively. He nodded. "Good night, Edith."

"Good night, Geoffrey." She sounded like a child speaking to her nanny.

Geoffrey shut the door and came back to Colin. "I'll wish you a good night, sir." He bowed. "An' I mean that in a most non-lascivious way."

He went down the stairs, taking the lantern with him.

Colin waited until he'd gone through the door, hearing it shut and the valet's footsteps dying away as he left the porch and stepped into the yard. Through the windows he saw the lantern's light disappear around the lodge's corner. Most of the wall lamps were burning low now, and he stood in semi-darkness. He took a step toward the master bedchamber door, then rapped gently on its surface. Without waiting for an answer, he opened the door and went in.

Chapter 19

Fiona stood near the bed. She was wrapped in a frothy concoction reminding him of nothing more than a swathe of whipped cream bedecked with sugar rosebuds. *Like th' ones on our weddin' cake*, he decided. That made a sudden dampness in his mouth. Colin swallowed and immediately went dry.

Her hair was unbound, waving down her back in a fall of curls, except for several tangles about her ears and forehead. She was the most beautiful creature he'd ever seen and he told her so.

She smiled demurely, whispered, "Thank you…"

…and threw herself at him.

There was no other way to describe that forward lunge as her arms went around his neck and her body struck his. Colin staggered backward, crashing against the door and making it slam shut under their combined weights. He had a moment's worry what Edith might think if she'd heard that, then Fiona kissed him, covering his face with feverish caresses.

He managed to gain his balance, turning his head long enough to ask, "So you're glad t' see me?"

Her answer to that was to kiss him again, this time on the mouth.

"Well now, Mrs. McCoy," he gasped. "When did you become so bold?"

"Since that title was placed before my name." She

kissed him one more time.

"You mean, that's all it took t' unleash this fantastic show o' affection?" Colin's arms closed around her and he swung her off the floor. "Lord!"

There followed several more shows of mutual affection, kisses, growing stronger by the minute, hands traveling and touching previously forbidden places. Fiona's lips opened, Colin thrust his tongue inside. There was only the barest hesitation before she returned the favor, her own, warm and damp, followed his back into his own mouth, where it searched, found, and entwined.

He set her down, releasing her. She slid her hands down his chest.

"My God, Fiona. I ne'er dreamed… Here now, what are you doin'?

One hand pulled at the neck of his nightshirt, plucking open a button. He put a hand over her fingers, then asked himself why he was stopping her.

"I'm trying to get you out of this thing." She made it sound so reasonable. "Why are you wearing it anyway?" She looked up at him. "I had Edith ask Geoffrey if you wore nightshirts and he told her it was none of her business."

Colin couldn't imagine shy little Edith asking his valet such a thing or Fiona telling her to do so. "For th' same reason, you're wearin' that nightgown, I imagine…because naithur o' us should've been bare before our servants t'night."

"The servants are gone now, so we don't need these things." She got one button open and started on the second.

"Lass, wait." Colin stepped out of reach.

Her eager fingers fell.

"Are you that impatient?" He couldn't believe it. "I mean, from all I've heard o' weddin' nights, th' bride's supposed t' be shy an' retirin' an'...I don't know...ignorant. If you'll pardon me sayin' so, you seem...well...full o' knowledge, somehow...?"

He made it a question, without actually intending to.

She took a deep breath. He wondered if he'd insulted her, or...God forbid...she wasn't as innocent as he thought.

"I *am* ignorant." She made it a simple declaration of fact and nowhere near a confession. "But I don't want to stay that way. I know absolutely nothing of what's to happen between us tonight, Colin, except that you're to exercise your husbandly rights, whatever those may be." She shrugged. "Not even my mother's seen fit to enlighten me and I didn't dare ask my father. However, turnabout is fair play and I sincerely hope there are wifely rights, also."

The look she gave him was quite earnest, her eyes meeting his squarely without shifting and, surprisingly, no blush.

"I want to know what goes on in a marriage bed, Colin. I'm so tired of wondering why my married friends get together and giggle and then fall silent when I appear. I know they're sharing secrets I've no right to know, but now..."

She gave a little cry of exasperation.

"Do you know...I've never seen a man's bare foot and certainly not his leg, except at the lake when someone dared appear in one of those bathing suits. Yours..." She looked down, staring at Colin's slippered feet. "Let me see your feet."

Obediently, he toed off his slippers. She stared.

"You have beautiful feet."

For some odd reason, that made him blush.

Me clodhoppers? Beautiful? He glanced down, seeing nothing but long, narrow feet and big hairy toes. *Is she lookin' at th' same trotters I am?*

"And your legs...what I can see of them..." She dared catch the hem of his nightshirt between thumb and forefinger and pull it to one side. "Let me see the rest of you, Colin. Show me that mystery that's always hidden inside a man's trousers." She caught the neck of Colin's nightshirt, wrenching it apart. Buttons went flying. "I've a right now and I...want...to...know!"

"In that case, you will." Colin again pulled the shirt from her grasp. "But..."

She waved her hands, then let them fall.

"We'll both take off our sleepwear." He finished opening the remaining buttons. "At th' same time."

Fiona pulled open the ruffled yoke of her own gown, revealing a curve of white bosom. Colin felt his cock jerk, knew if he looked down, it might actually be peeping out the Glory Hole, struggling to get a better view.

"Colin, what's that...?" Fiona had seen also.

"Part o' th' mystery, lass."

He unbuttoned his cuffs. She did the same, untying the ribbons holding her sleeves closed.

"On th' count o' three, we'll shed e'erything." He took a deep breath. "Ready?"

She nodded. Her bosom was heaving. Colin wondered if his own breathing was as fast and labored. His heart was beating so rapidly he couldn't tell.

"One...two...three!"

He bent and seized the hem of the nightshirt, pulling

it up and over his head. As he surfaced from its enveloping folds, he saw a white garment sail past, landing in a frothy heap on the floor.

Fiona stood there, bare, pale, and beautiful. Colin's nightshirt slid from his fingers.

"Oh, lass…"

She took a step toward him. They came together at the edge of the bed, flesh colliding with flesh, warmth against heat, a firm male body against a softer female one that was no less demanding and eager.

"Show me all there is, husband," Fiona murmured.

Colin looked down. Her breasts were crushed against his chest, nipples pink and rounded against his skin, belly and thighs ground to his. All the things he'd thought, had been prepared to do and say went flying out the window.

She wants me an' I want her an' that's all there is t' it.

"Don't worry, me wife. I'm goin' ta."

With that, he lifted her to the bed and fell into its soft depths beside her.

Chapter 20

It was nearly noon before Colin and Fiona appeared the next day. Though scents floating from below told them Geoffrey had returned and prepared breakfast, no one disturbed them by knocking on the door and announcing the meal was ready. Apparently, knowing when to be silent and invisible was also taught to valets.

Footsteps and voices announced the footman, coachman, and Edith ate their own breakfasts and then dispersed. Colin wondered briefly what they were doing, then dismissed it because he didn't care. If Edith had been older, he might've guessed she and Geoffrey were having their own little bed-party, but he had faith his valet wouldn't take advantage of someone that much younger. The sound of the front door closing and a single pair of footsteps going upstairs to Edith's room confirmed this.

From that point on, the world could've disappeared, as well as everyone in it. He and Fiona were alone, isolated—Adam and Eve of their own domain—not caring who or what existed outside their bedchamber door.

Fiona had been more than eager to learn all there was; Colin had been just as ready to teach her. From the moment their bodies touched, there was no awkwardness between them. There was a single painful hesitation at the beginning, but Colin held her while she sobbed slightly.

Fiona wiped her tears, sighed, and said, "Now I'm truly yours, Colin McCoy, and I'm going to make certain you never want anyone else."

"Darlin', I ne'er will, believe me," he swore and began to make love to her in earnest.

After that first time, he was breathless, and in the midst of his recovery, Donal's admonition came to him. *If it happens, it's incidental, braithur. I'm not doin' this for me, nor me family. If a babe comes from it, well an' good, but for now… 'tis only t' show me wife how much I care.*

They played, they teased, touched, kissed, and caressed. Colin thought no woman he'd ever been with, though there truly hadn't been that many in his eight-and-twenty years, had pleased him, satisfied him, as this one had, this woman whom he'd chosen as the one to become his only lawful wife…his Fiona.

Chapter 21

When Colin opened the door preparing to run across the landing and fetch his clothing from that other bedroom where he'd changed, he discovered his portmanteau standing by the door.

Good ol' Geoff strikes again.

He brought it inside and proceeded to let his bride watch her husband prepare his toilette. Shaving was a bit of a problem because she kept getting between him and the mirror, kissing him and getting lather on her face, making him drop his razor into the basin.

At last, he kissed her and said, "Get out o' th' way, lass, before you make me accidentally cut me throat…an wouldn't that be a bit o' a bad way t' end our weddin' happiness?"

She sat on the bed while he shaved, washed his face free of soap, then got dressed. Afterward, he helped her into her stays and all the other female *accoutrements*, making facetious comments and kissing every inch of flesh as it was hidden from view.

"You're a good lady's maid," she commented.

"At your service, me lady." He bowed.

"You certainly have been." She kissed him and laughed. "I suppose I shall have to be careful in what I say now, for I daren't speak something like that before others. Oh, Colin, how I wish I were able to walk into a room and declare how wonderful you are in bed!" She giggled. "Wouldn't that shock everyone? And make all the women envy me?" She looked thoughtful. "And all the men envy *you*. To have your wife tell the world of your ability?"

"An' that would be th' greatest scandal e'er," he agreed. "Best keep it our li'l secret, love." He placed a finger over her lips. "Something for us t' enjoy all t' ourselves. Now then." He whirled her around, checking that all buttons and hooks were closed. "Are we ready, Mrs. McCoy?"

"That we are, Mr. McCoy."

With that, he offered her his arm. Fiona placed her hand on his forearm. Colin opened the door and they walked out onto the landing.

****

"Geoffrey, I had no idea you were such a good cook," Fiona declared as she patted her lips with a napkin.

"Indeed, Mistress, a good valet knows how t' do a bit o' everythin'." Geoffrey gathered the dishes.

"When you marry, your wife is going to get a well-rounded husband," she said.

"Ah, I don't think I'll be takin' that route, ma'am." Geoffrey shook his head. He added Colin's plate to the stack.

"Why not?" Fiona asked.

"There would be too much mournin' in th' world if I chose only one woman." Geoffrey picked up the plates and hurried away to the kitchen. "'Twill only take a moment an' then we'll be ready t' go, sir."

"Was he serious?" Fiona asked, in a loud whisper.

Colin shrugged. "Sometimes with Geoffrey, 'tis difficult t' tell."

"Colin, is your valet a rake?"

"Fiona, if that were so, I'd have t' be a rake, too."

She looked thoughtful and started to speak.

"Don't ask," he said quickly.

****

They entered the coach and soon were on their way to the railway station. From there, they took a train to Dublin's port, to set sail in a packet for England and on to Paris.

Edith was all agog at going abroad. Geoffrey took it in stride. He'd traveled with Quinton and Colin when Colin went on his Grand Tour, so this was nothing new. He kept the little maid entertained with tales of the things he'd seen on that trip, and her mind off the seasickness threatening to creep upon her from time to time. Fiona and Colin however were too much involved with each other to be offset by *mal-de-mer*.

Colin did only one thing he hadn't planned while he was in Paris. He wrote Padraig.

Padraig Aloysius Francis McCoy

The Shamrock Ranch

McCoy's Crossing, Nebraska Territory

United States of America

Dear Brother:

Congratulate me. I'm married.

There, that's plain and short enough. As you can see by the postmark, I'm in Paris on my wedding trip. I love her dearly.

That's all I wish to say.

Your loving brother who occasionally misses you and wishes you were here,

Colin Uilliam Conchobhar McCoy

Currently residing in Paris

Chapter 22

Two weeks later, they were back in Tipperary where Colin and Fiona both affected a bored attitude when in public while hiding a frantic passion they unleashed only in private. They caused quite a shock their first night at McCoy Hall, when Colin announced Fiona would be sharing his bedroom so the one given her would be unnecessary. Subsequently, it was kept shut and visited by a maid once a month to dust and that was all.

As promised, Colin settled in earnest into clerking for his father, relieving Quinton of that chore. For him, the work wasn't difficult and he often finished so early he and Fiona had time to be alone, whether it was to go for a ride or a picnic, or simply to disappear into their bedchamber for an hour or two. After Donald's revelation of Felicity's injury, however, Colin soon discontinued riding, and whenever he and Fiona went out, it was always by carriage or shay. He wasn't going to risk anything happening to *his* wife as had happened to his brother's.

****

Three months after their return from Paris, Fiona complained of feeling ill. She spent the entire day in bed, with a headache. The next day, the carriage was brought round and she and Edith rode into town to see the McCoy family doctor. When she returned, she sent Edith on her way and went directly to the study where Colin was poring over one of the account books.

"May I interrupt you?"

"Certainly, love. Figures don't bother me like they do Da, but I always welcome an interruption from you." He thought she looked pale. "What did th' doctor say? Some pesty fever or such come up from th' river? Are we all going t' have t' dose ourselves with sulphur and molasses?" He laughed. "I hope not. I hate that partic'lar concoction."

"I'm afraid what's wrong with me can't be cured with sulphur and molasses," Fiona said, and immediately blushed a brilliant pink. "It certainly won't be affecting *you*, either."

"What does that mean?" he demanded, getting up and going to her. "Fiona, what's th' matter?" Abruptly, he was worried. "You were pale an' now you're so red-faced. Is it…" He searched his mind for what might cause such a change in complexion. "'Tisn't your heart?"

"It's my heart, all right." Her smile calmed him some, while also worrying him. "It's about to burst, with joy, and fear. Colin…oh Colin…"

A tear trickled down her cheek and she began to sob.

"Here now. What is it?" Gently, Colin put his arms around her and led her to a nearby settee. He sat beside her, pulling her close. "Whate'er 'tis, sweetheart, we'll get th' best doctors an' you'll get well, I promise."

"I only want Dr. Hyde," she said, brushing at her eyes.

"But he's no specialist…"

"I don't need a specialist. Colin. I'm not ill."

"Then why those tears? Why…"

"I'm going to have a baby, Colin."

He didn't speak for perhaps three seconds. When he

did, he said the most stupid thing anyone could utter. "A baby? Whose?"

She stared at him for the space of a single breath before her hand came up and she struck him on the shoulder. "Yours, you foolish man. Whose do you think?"

"Sorry, I guess that was a silly thing t' say. I'm not thinkin'…a baby…I…Oh, damn, Fiona…Oh, God…"

I did it! His thoughts became a frenzied frazzle to cover his shock and his happiness. Because he had no idea what to say, he simply sat there, hugging her until Fiona pushed him away.

"Are you happy, Colin? I know it's soon, but…"

"Happy? You can't imagine how much." He was also a bit dismayed that'd he'd obeyed his brother's command too well.

Three months married and still not truly accustomed to having her small body sleeping next to his, nor of having a wife to make love to whenever he wanted, and now…they'd created another being who would steal Fiona from him within nine months' time. Nay, sooner than that, because as her girth grew…

No matter, Colin told himself. *We'll make time for each ithir. Somehow. Da an' Mama did, an' there were four o' us.* He forced himself to be optimistic. *We'll always make time t' be alone. I swear.*

****

Once he'd recovered and accepted the fact he was to be a father, Fiona asked him to wait a few more months before informing Quinton. Colin agreed, but felt duty-bound to write Donal right away. He did that without telling Fiona, one of the few times he'd do anything without informing her beforehand, the other time being an absolute life-changer for both.

****

Donal Callum Seamus McCoy, Esquire
3 Elm Tree Mews, Sedley House
London, England
The United Kingdom of Great Britain
Dear Donal:

I am writing this letter to inform you I have accomplished the mission you set before me on my wedding day. Neither Father nor anyone else has been informed yet, so please keep it quiet. You may tell Felicity, of course, if you choose. We plan to announce the joyous event to everyone in a few more months.

You can stop worrying about the family name.

I am now floundering in the throes of expectant fatherhood.

Your brother,
Coilin Uilliam Conchobhar McCoy
McCoy Hall
Tipperary, Ireland
The United Kingdom of Great Britain

Chapter 23

Winter, 1861

Uilliam Coilin Fionn McCoy was born nine months to the day after the date of their arrival in Paris. The weather now was crisp and cold. There had been a new snowfall two nights before and the fires were roaring in all the hearths.

Colin's fears to the contrary, Fiona experienced a fairly uneventful pregnancy. She carried on so normally until around the seventh month that he occasionally expressed doubts she was with child at all.

Fiona's reply to that was a very unladylike snort and the statement, "Do you truly believe I have always liked fried pigs' trotters with apple slices? Or lemon curd with quince jelly? Truly, Colin, I hope you're joking."

Colin had retorted that he thought those taste combinations a bit odd, but was hoping she'd liked such things all along and simply hadn't mentioned them until now.

At that, Fiona gave him a look that should've knocked him to the floor. She gathered her sewing and joined his mother in the parlor where they proceeded to make yet another little gown for the baby.

"Which also points to its existence," she added.

Around two o'clock that fateful morning, Fiona woke Colin from a deep snore. They'd fallen asleep in each other's arms, Colin vowing even if he couldn't make love to his wife now, he was going to be as close to her as possible while they slept.

The fact that he'd gone with Quinton that day to collect the rents probably added to his exhaustion. They'd ridden over a good portion of County Tipperary before returning home.

"Colin...Colin!"

Her call finally broke through his sawing and snorting.

"Sorry, lass," he muttered, exhaling noisily. "Me snorin' gettin' t' you?"

Fiona had never complained of his snoring, though he asked her occasionally. She replied that once she got to sleep, he could've fired off a cannon and she wouldn't hear. Colin was thankful for that and hoped she wasn't telling him a lie.

He rolled over and drifted back to sleep. When she continued shaking him, however, he woke, sat up, and looked around. She seized his arm in an iron grasp.

"What is it?"

"Colin..." She stopped, gasped, and squeezed his arm tighter.

"Damn, Fiona, that hurt. Why are you clutchin' me arm so?" He leaned over and turned the key on the lamp, making the flame higher. His voice went up as he saw her face. "You're cryin'. Sweet, what's th' matter?"

"Colin..." Her hand slid from his arm to the bulge of her belly. "The baby..."

"Is th' li'l fella kickin' again?" That was one of Colin's great joys, to feel the child move beneath the delicate shell of its mother's belly. "I swear th' lad's goin' t be a champion dancer..." He broke off as Fiona

Toni V. Sweeney

gasped and bit her lip.

Colin placed a hand on her belly. It seemed to move in long, slow ripples beneath his fingers.

"That's no kick… What…" Understanding dawned. "Oh, Fiona…nay…"

"Oh, Colin, yes." Her hands went to her back. "He's coming, Colin, and I think it'll be soon."

Throwing back the covers, Colin nearly fell from the bed. He recovered and ran to the door.

Before he could get it open, Fiona called, "Colin! At least put on your robe." The last word ended in a near shriek as another pain struck.

Finding his dressing gown, he threw it on, looked around frantically for his slippers, couldn't find them, and flung open the door, sending it rebounding against the wall. In bare feet, he ran from the room, down the hall, and straight to Quinton's door.

"Da!" He battered the door with both fists. It visibly shuddered under his touch. He struck it again. "Da!"

"Colin, what in hell…" Quinton jerked open the door. His hair, tousled from sleep, stood up in tangled red curls, hanging in his face. "'Tis two o'clock, lad, what…"

"'Tis th' babe, Da. 'Tis comin'." With that, Colin ran back to his bedroom. "I've got t' get dressed an' ride for Dr. Hyde."

"Nay," Quinton called after him. "We'll send one o' th' footmen. You stay with Fiona." He hurried back inside to pull on a pair of trousers over his nightshirt, get his own dressing gown, and go to Màiri's room.

He always thought women were lighter sleepers than men. When his wife was at the door after his first soft knock, that confirmed it.

194

"I heard," she said before he could speak. "Get Colin out of there. If he's anything like you were, he'll make the poor lass more frantic than she already is."

Tying the belt of her wrapper, she bustled past.

"I've rung for Edith. We'll take over until the doctor gets here." She stopped, looking back. "You've rung for Cormac and told him to fetch one of the footmen, haven't you?"

"Of course," Quinton lied. He followed his wife into the bedroom where Fiona was huddled in the bed with Colin holding her in his arms.

"Colin, dear." Màiri caught her son's arm, pulling him from the bed despite his protests, while Quinton stealthily sidled to the hearth and tugged on the bellpull next to the mantel. "Get yourself dressed and go downstairs with your da. Let me take over."

"But I can't leave…"

"Nay. You're going to be no good here now. This is women's work, and the doctor's."

Fiona gave her a grateful glance while the one she turned on Colin held relief. Màiri wondered what he'd been saying to her as he attempted to calm her.

Still protesting, Colin gathered scattered clothing and was dragged from the room by Quinton, shirt and trousers draped over his arm. He put them on while they waited in the parlor as Cormac appeared and was instructed to get a footman on the road to the doctor's.

****

As births went, it was quick, and easy…or so Colin was told. As far as he was concerned, all the screams and cries coming from that bedchamber were the most horrendous he'd ever heard.

As a youngster, Colin had been present when a

couple of his father's mares foaled, allowed by his father and the groom to attend. By accident, he'd seen one or two cows calve in the pastures, but neither of those events had prepared him for the birth of his own son.

"God, Da...I-I thought it'd be like with th' mares. She sounds like she's dyin'. Naithur o' th' horses made such sounds..." White-faced, Colin accepted the brandy Quinton offered, gulping it down and then choking as its heat seared his throat. He coughed and turned a stricken face to his father. "Have I killed her, Da? Is Fiona going t' die because I put this babe in her?"

"Calm down, lad." Quinton took a swallow of his own brandy. "I know it sounds awful, but 'twas th' same way when you an' th' ithirs were born." He gave a short bark of a laugh. "Seems it's a lot more painful t' bring a child into this world than it is t' create one."

"I suppose I should be thankful for that," Colin muttered, taking a smaller swallow of brandy this time. As another scream floated down the stairs, he briefly envied Donal, who'd never have to hear such cries. "Else, there wouldn't be many o' us humans, would there?"

Sudden quiet followed.

"Mr. Colin?" A timid call from the parlor door made both look up.

A very white-faced Edith stood in the doorway, eyes red with tear-tracks. She'd been too frightened to tell Màiri this was the first time she'd ever been present during a birth and had silently sobbed in sympathy with her mistress as she ran around the bedchamber doing what she was ordered. She was holding something clutched to her little bosom.

"What is it? Is that...?" Colin jumped to his feet,

running barefoot to her. He still hadn't found his slippers.

She held out the bundle and Colin snatched it from her, fumbling with the folds, uncovering what lay inside. He stared.

"Oh, Da…" The face he raised to Quinton's was stark white. A tear slid out of the corner of his eye and trickled down his cheek.

Quinton put his arm across Colin's shoulders to steady him. He thought his son looked as if he were well on the way to fainting. He looked down at his grandchild.

"He's perfect, lad, an' a true McCoy. Look at that red hair." He considered, then asked, "It *is* a son?"

Edith nodded, while Colin continued to stare at the baby. Opening the blanket further, he confirmed his father's question as he counted fingers and toes, balancing the baby awkwardly against his chest while he touched little arms and legs. His son was small but looked perfectly formed as far as he could tell. The baby woke, waved a fist in protest at his father's awkward manhandling. He made a sound like a kitten's mew, then opened his eyes, looked up at the shape hovering above him and began to shriek.

"Why's he cryin?" Colin clutched the child tighter, eliciting more screams. "What did I do?"

"He wants his ma, I'm thinkin'," Edith snatched the baby from him, rewrapping it in the blanket as she hurried out the door.

"Nay, wait, Edith." Colin pursued her, protesting, "Stop!"

"Let her go, son." Quinton's hand on his shoulder prevented Colin's rush to the stairs. Edith scurried up them.

"You'll be seein' th' lad from now on, until you get sick o' him."

"Ne'er," Colin declared. "I'll ne'er get tired o' him, no more than you did us, Da."

"An' who says I ne'er got weary o' havin' so many li'l ones underfoot?" Quinton demanded. He laughed as Colin turned a shocked look on him. "Ah, I'm joshin', lad. I love all o' you, an' I'm lookin' forward t' there bein' a li'l one in th' house again."

He turned Colin and guided him back into the parlor.

"Come in an' relax an' let's drink a toast t' th' newest McCoy. Then, after Fiona's recovered a bit an' th' doctor says 'tis all right, you can see *her,* too."

****

When Colin did see Fiona, he rushed to her bedside, grasping her hands and kissing them frantically. She was propped against three feather pillows, hands resting on the covers pulled up to her breast.

"Oh, sweetheart."

"I want you to know right now." Her voice was surprisingly strong for one looking so pale and washed out. "Kissing my hands is all you're going to be doing for quite some time, Mr. Colin McCoy."

"What?" He stared at her as if he didn't understand.

"You heard me." She sat up, pulling her hands from his. "Do you think I want to go through this again anytime soon?"

"B-but, Fiona…" Colin was glad they were alone in the bedroom. He wouldn't have wanted anyone else to hear that. "Sweetheart…"

His confusion increased as she began to laugh.

"Oh…oh, if only you could see your face." She put both hands to her mouth, chuckling loudly. "Oh, dearest, you looked so stricken."

"You—you were jokin'?"

"Truly, I couldn't resist."

"Well, thank you, wife," Anger took the place of confusion. "Here I sat downstairs worryin' about you an' fearin' for your life...an' ignorin' me child's fate...an' you decide t' jest with me? T' give yourself a bit o' a giggle?"

"Oh, Colin, please, don't be angry." She caught his hands, copying his own gesture as she kissed his palm. "I was teasing. It came to me when you rushed in, all worry and concern...how much I loved you, but after what I'd gone through, I shouldn't...not at all. Truly I should wish to keep you at arm's length for years. I apologize."

Sighing, she brushed an errant curl out of his eyes. In it, Colin thought he heard the remembrance of all that pain.

"It was cruel. Will you forgive me?"

"Well..." He turned his hand so it tightened around hers. "It's glad I am that you feel well enough to joke about it, but... Perhaps we'll be a bit more cautious from now on. Maybe schedule th' next babe a long time later?"

"That would be a splendid idea," she agreed. "Is there a way to do that?"

He looked around, making certain no one was standing in the hallway to hear, since he'd left the door open and wasn't going to leave her to shut it. His father and mother were downstairs sharing a glass of wine with the doctor before he went on his way.

Colin whispered, "'Tis a secret we men know. I'll share it with you, darlin', an' the lad there'll be our only one until we're ready for th' next."

"What shall we call him?"

For the first time, Colin realized that in all their talk about the child, they'd never discussed a name. "I'd like t' name him after meself."

"Coilin Uilliam Conchobhar?"

"Not exactly in that order, but Uilliam Coilin," he corrected. "An' also after you, Fiona. Uilliam Coilin Fionn. Unless you've some objection."

She shook her head.

Colin got to his feet and walked over to the crib. Sometime, during all that was happening, someone had brought it from the nursery. Inside, the baby was asleep.

"Guess we'd better enjoy these quiet moments while we can. I'd pick him up, but then he'd probably wake, an'… He cried when he saw me. I don't think he likes me, Fiona." He laughed and it was a slightly wry sound. "I hope he doesn't hold that attitude fore'er."

The baby opened its eyes.

"He doesn't seem t' be cryin' now. Maybe…" Colin bent and scooped the child out of the cradle.

Someone had dressed him in a white gown, one of those Colin remembered seeing Fiona laboring over. He looked like a little china doll.

"Well, now, Uilliam Coilin Fionn McCoy. Welcome to the family." Lowering his voice, Colin whispered, "I love you, Liam, me son. Truly."

Carrying the baby to the bed, he sat on its edge, placing him in Fiona's arms. Liam wiggled a bit, then closed his eyes and went back to sleep.

"I'm going t' be a good faithur, Fiona," Colin whispered. He touched one of the little hands with just his finger. The baby's own fingers closed around it.

Colin kissed the delicate little wrist.

"I know you will, Colin," she said. "You'll be as good a father as Father Quinton is."

That was what she'd begun calling Quinton when they returned from Paris, following Felicity in that respect. It always made Colin smile to hear it. He laughed out loud now.

"Oh, aye. At least as good as Faithur Quinton, if not better."

Chapter 24

Padraig Aloysius Francis McCoy, Esquire
The Shamrock Ranch
McCoy's Crossing, Nebraska Territory
United States of America
Dear Brother:
It is my pride and pleasure to announce the birth of my son Uillliam Coilin Fionn. Don't bother counting backwards. He was born within the legal and accepted time for a first infant and I'll have none of your wondering on that score. I simply worked a bit faster than I expected, that's all.

I wished to let you know of my good fortune.

Please give my regards to your wife and tell her she is now an aunt.

Your brother,
Coilin Uilliam Conchobhar McCoy
McCoy Hall
Tipperary, Ireland
The United Kingdom of Great Britain

Chapter 25

A week after his birth, Liam was christened, with his parents, both sets of grandparents, and his aunt Bridget and uncles Samuel and Donal in attendance. Phelan Foyle, now courting one of Fiona's cousins, was asked to stand as godfather while Felicity's maternal cousin Charity was asked to be godmother. Great-uncle Seamus, because of his age, was unable to attend, as was third cousin Connell who had to care for him. Liam was quiet and well-behaved, looking more than ever like a china cherub, in his long white christening robes, adorned with lace and white ribbons, wispy curls a carroty halo surrounding his head. Well-behaved until the moment the priest poured the baptismal water, that is.

Giving a terrific shriek, Liam bawled and didn't stop until the ceremony was completed. As the concerned adults gathered around, cooing and attempting to calm him, he gave a final sob and sniffle and fell silent.

"Oh, he was so frightened," Màiri sympathized.

Liam stared at her out of cloudy tear-filled eyes.

"Yes, you were, weren't you, darling…all that cold water on your little head?"

"Now there, I think you're mistaken, Mama." Colin laughed. "I'm wonderin' exactly how much o' that was real fright an' how much simply theatrics t' keep our attention. T' me way o' thinkin', he seemed more angry than anythin' else…that someone would dare do such a thin' t' Master Liam McCoy."

Liam's birth wrought several changes in the McCoy household, not the least of which was that Colin was now accepted as a full-fledged adult member of the family. The servants no longer regarded him as they had when he was a child, an adolescent, or even a young adult, with that fond but slightly patronizing air hinting they thought whatever he said was mostly butterflies and balderdash. Quinton came to him with matters of running the estate as well as his duties as steward for Alisdaire. He was now treated with a surprising respect by the townsfolk, as if by becoming a father, he shed some unseen and unspoken onus that had hovered over him.

Perhaps it was that he'd now established he was in no respect like Padraig whom all still remembered as a womanizer and a wastrel, in spite of the information Quinton always relayed if anyone asked of his second-born son.

If the father was now completely accepted, the son was spoiled beyond all doubt. When his Uncle Donal and Aunt Felicity came to visit, they brought trunks of toys and books, anything and everything catching their eyes they thought a child would love. They bestowed on their nephew the love they would've given their own child.

As far as anyone was concerned, Liam was the crown prince of the McCoy family. It didn't matter that Bridget and her husband had six children. Liam was the first grandchild bearing the McCoy name and therefore was important for that reason, if for no other. He was spoiled, coddled, and loved…and his father was hard put on occasion to punish him when he misbehaved, which was often because he was pampered so.

In spite of that, as he grew older, the little boy became a fairly well-behaved child, as if sensing his importance but deciding not to take advantage of it.

When Liam was a few months old, a package arrived from Nebraska. It was addressed to *Master Uilliam C.F. McCoy.*

"What can it be, do you suppose?" Colin, sitting at his desk with his son braced against his knee, turned the brown-paper-wrapped box around and around in his free hand. "Is it somethin' from your Uncle Padraig do you think, Liam?"

Liam merely continued to suck his fist, drooling onto his father's knee. He was dressed in a blue gown, its hem, nearly twelve inches longer than his legs, adorned with lace on collar and yoke.

Colin thought it a bit dandified for a boy-child, in spite of the color, but it was a gift from Godmother Charity, so Liam wore it, nevertheless.

"Oh, Colin, let me take him so you can open it." Fiona held out her hands.

"Nay, let the lad be." Colin waved her away. "'Tis his package an' he needs t' be here when 'tis opened."

"You can't do it with one hand," Fiona pointed out, practically. She took the box from him. "Shall I?"

"I think you're as curious as I an' simply can't wait," Colin accused. "Go ahead. I admit, I'm curious t' see what Padraig's sent our boy."

Using the letter opener on the desk, Fiona cut through the string binding the package, then tore away the wrapping. Inside was a small box with a letter tied around it. Fiona pulled the letter free and set it aside. She opened the box.

It was lined with white tissue paper. She pushed it

aside. On a small velvet cushion was a feather, fashioned out of silver.

She took it out of the box. "It's a stickpin." She twirled it so it caught the light and glittered.

Liam laughed and took his fist out of his mouth, holding it out, trying to reach the pin.

"No, dear, I don't think you need this, just yet. When you get older, you may wear it. Yes, with your first cravat. It'll look very nice." She studied the pin, noting the detail in the engraved lines. "It's certainly realistic enough. Do you suppose it's real silver?"

"Probably. I've no idea what precious metals they have in that country, but Padraig was always a bit o' a spendthrift. I doubt he'd stint on his nephew's christenin' gift." Colin held out his hand. "Hand me th' letter."

Fiona opened it, placing it in his hand. He read a few lines and laughed. "Guess I'd better read this out loud since 'tis address t' you, son." He cleared his throat.

Master Uilliam Coilin Fionn McCoy
McCoy Hall
Tipperary, Ireland
The United Kingdom of Great Britain
My dear nephew,
Enclosed you will find a small gift I hope arrived in time for your christening, but if not, please excuse that.

It's an eagle feather, fashioned by a member of the Lakota tribe who live near my ranch. They consider the eagle a very important bird, believing it is the master of the sky, closer to God than any other creature. To present someone an eagle feather is to give him the highest respect and love because the eagle represents honour, truth, wisdom, and courage.

Wear this feather with pride, lad, and whenever you

do, know that, as far away as I am, I love you, nephew.
May it set you on an honourable path and keep you there.
    Your uncle,
    Padraig Aloysius Francis McCoy
    The Shamrock Ranch
    McCoy's Crossing, Nebraska Territory
    United States of America

"I'll put it away for now," Fiona decided, "and when he's older, I know he'll be proud to wear it."

Colin looked thoughtful. In that moment, he wished more than anything he could see his brother again.

Chapter 26

Liam McCoy seemed to be blessed. He went through his first three years with never a mishap or serious illness. Those childhood sicknesses he did suffer were the mildest cases possible and the doctor declared his surprise at that. Fiona had pinned Padraig's stickpin to the lining at the head of Liam's crib and stated his uncle's gift kept him safe. She noted often the baby would look at the pin while he lay in his crib, watching the sunshine reflect off its gleaming surface.

Shortly after Liam turned two, Fiona told Colin she wanted another baby.

"You're certain?" He looked doubtful, as if she didn't know what she was saying. "Didn't I hear you just th' other day lamentin' what a handful Liam is?" He thought a moment. "Aye, that time he chased one o' th' huntin' hounds through th' kitchen an' tripped th' scully, makin' her spill th' cake batter."

"That was a mere prank." Fiona, like everyone else, made excuses where Liam was concerned. "High spirits. After I explained that he might've hurt Ellen and we wouldn't have cake for tea that day because the batter was ruined and there no more eggs, he was apologetic. Yes, Colin, I think it's time we had another baby. You did say you wanted Liam to have at least one brother, didn't you?"

"He might have a sister," Colin pointed out, "but

that'd be good. Then, he'd learn early on how he has t' treat young ladies."

He nodded and caught Fiona around the waist, swinging her off the floor.

"Very well, me dear. Can't say I won't be glad t' stop usin' that preventive. We'll try again an' hope for anaithur son. Shall we call this one after your braithur?"

****

When Colin rode round the county with his father, collecting the rents and inspecting the farms or meeting with tenants who had complaints, more times than not Liam rode with them, perched on the front of his father's saddle. That worried Fiona, of course, who was certain he'd let the child fall and be trampled by his horse.

Colin swore that would never happen and teased her with the idea of making a carrier for Liam.

"…like those Indian women use. They put their babies in kind o' knapsacks an' carry them on their backs."

"How do you know about that?" Fiona asked, suspicious he was fabricating such a fact.

"I read about it in a book," Colin answered. "One written by an American. *Th' History o' th' Expedition Under th' Command o' th' Captains Lewis an' Clark* by Meriwether Lewis. He was some kind o' explorer."

"Where did you find such a book?"

"'Twas in th' library. I've no idea where it came from because I didn't think Da was interested in America at all, but that's where it was…stuck back on a top shelf." Colin looked thoughtful. "I enjoyed it. I must ask Da where he got it. Maybe 'twas Donal's. He's th' history expert."

In the end, Fiona managed to convince Colin not to

Toni V. Sweeney

take Liam on any more rides until the boy was old enough to ride his own pony.

That's probably why, when Liam was three, Father Christmas left a fat Shetland pony named Pudge in the stables for him, though Fiona managed to delay his receiving riding instructions for another year while the pony frolicked in the meadow and got even fatter.

Chapter 27

When Liam was nearly four, he learned how to swim, in spite of Fiona's protests.

Colin had come into the nursery where Liam was having his bath, splashing and rolling about in the little tin tub. Fiona insisted on bathing the child herself and had sent the nursemaid on other chores. Occasionally, Colin attended, adding to Liam's mischief by encouraging the child to splash and play while Fiona attempted to wash his face and ears.

"Oh, you're like a little fish, Uilliam Coilin," she exclaimed. "Stop that splashing. Look, you're gotten Mama's dress soaked." She lifted her skirts slightly, sending water rolling off her lap onto the floor.

Liam merely laughed and splashed more water. He lay back in the tub and kicked even harder, sending water flying, then picked up the soap and began to dip it into and out of the water.

"You're a li'l fish all right," Colin agreed. "But fish don't kick, son. They wiggle their fins, an'..." He stopped. "Fiona, I've just had a thought."

"Do I dare ask what?" Fiona lifted a dripping Liam from the tub and set him on the towel in her lap. She took the soap from him, replaced it in its dish, and began to dry the child.

"Liam needs t' know how t' swim. Don't know why I didn't think o' this sooner."

"And he can learn," Fiona answered, blotting Liam's face with the towel. The child dodged. "Be still," she told him. "When he's a little older," she went on.

"Nay, he should know *now*," Colin insisted.

"Colin, he's barely four. Three and a half if we want to be precise," she protested.

"Which is big enough t' go wanderin' 'round th' stables an' who knows where else if someone isn't keepin' an eye on him." He looked shocked. "Fiona, he could fall into a horse trough an' drown."

"Oh surely…"

"Nay, 'tis true. A grown man could drown in one o' those things if he fell in and hit his head, an' a child…" Colin stood up. "I'm going t' teach him. Tomorrow."

"Where are you planning on doing this?" Fiona demanded. She wrapped Liam in the towel and carried him to his bed, setting him upon it. "Stay there while I get your nightshirt."

"Yes, Mama." For once, Liam obeyed. Sticking his thumb into his mouth, he sat quietly while Fiona rummaged through the chest's drawers.

"I'll take him t' th' pond," Colin replied, sounding as if he'd thought this out instead of it being a spur-of-the-moment idea. "That's where Da taught me, an' I was little more than four," he pointed out, as Fiona looked about to begin another protest. "He taught Padraig an' Donal there, too."

"Colin, I really don't think this is something having to be done…" Nightshirt in her hands, Fiona turned back to the bed. "Here we go!"

She dropped the nightshirt over the child's head, pulling his hands into the sleeves.

"Nay, Fiona, this is something needin' t' be done,

an' th' sooner th' better." Colin was adamant. "Liam, lad…" he said as Liam's bright head appeared in the neck of the nightshirt. "How'd you like t' go with your da t' th' pond tomorrow for a swim?"

"Do I have ta, Da?" The child had obviously been listening closely and decided to take his mother's side in the argument.

"I'm afraid you do, lad. Wouldn't you like t' know how t' swim so if you ever fall inta th' water, you won't…"

Fiona drew in a deep breath. Colin glanced at her. She shook her head.

"…have t' wait for your da or Granda Quinton t' pull you out?"

"It'll be fun," Fiona added, giving in and speaking in what she hoped was an encouraging voice not reflecting the way she felt.

"I guess." Liam didn't sound too certain, but if his mother was now enthusiastic about it…

"Good, then. We'll go there in th' morning."

Fiona sat on the bed beside Liam, biting her lip.

"…and Mama can come along, too, if she likes," Colin added. He laughed and squeezed Fiona's hand. "We'll have Cook pack us a lunch an' make a picnic o' it. After you learn t' swim, we'll eat. How about that?"

Liam, not seeing Fiona's attempt at a smile, nodded wholeheartedly. If food was included, he was always agreeable.

"Ah, thought that'd convince you, you li'l glutton!" Colin seized his son, pulling him from the bed and tossing him into the air, sending his nightshirt fluttering and revealing plump legs and a bare little bottom.

Chapter 28

The next morning, after breakfast and Liam's morning lessons—which at that time consisted of going over his ABC's, counting through numbers one to ten, and reciting a couple of nursery rhymes with his nanny— Colin, his son, and Fiona trudged down the slope behind McCoy Hall and followed the path through the trees to the pond.

It was a small pond as those bodies of water went, probably no more than thirty feet wide on a side, its depth at the deepest part only about eight feet, deep enough for a boat to float and a man to swim, but still dangerous for a near four-year-old. A small stream fed into it from the larger lake where Colin had taken Fiona and Edith in his curricle that now long-ago day, and that one in turn connected to the River Arra, eventually leading to the ocean.

There were fish in the pond and Liam was excited about that, asking Colin if he could catch some.

"When you can swim well enough t' keep up with a fish, you have me blessing t' catch all you want, son," his father promised.

Fiona continued being appropriately nervous as Colin undressed the little boy, carefully placing his clothing on a low-hanging branch of a pine tree. She'd spread a blanket on the grass under the tree and was attempting to sit quietly, with little success.

"He doesn't even have a bathing suit," she complained. "Colin, really...it's scandalous for you to take him into the water naked. I...Where's *your* suit?"

She realized her husband was also removing his own clothing and placing it beside his son's.

"Don't have one," he answered shortly as he folded his trousers and draped them over the limb before concentrating on his drawers. "You won't catch me wearin' one o' those silly-striped monkey suits."

"You won't be swimming in polite company, either," Fiona retorted.

"I don't particularly care ta." He turned to face her, placing his hands on his hips. At his side, Liam copied his action, chubby fists propped on fat little ribs.

"Oh!" Fiona put her hand over her eyes as if she couldn't bear the sight of all that male nakedness. She spread her fingers, peeping through them at her husband, thinking what a fine specimen he was, and how Liam was a miniature of his father.

Oh, the lasses are going to be in trouble when my boy gets older.

"I hope no one happens along."

"Don't worry, they won't." Colin took Liam's hand. "Come on, son, let's test th' water."

He led the child to the pond's edge, carefully dipping his toes into the water and wiggling them. Liam did the same.

"Seems all right, I'd say."

"Wight, Da," Liam agreed.

Colin waded in, tugging on Liam's hand. The child followed, at the last minute looking back at Fiona. Her expression made him hesitate.

"Da? Why's Mama look so sad?"

Colin glanced back. Fiona was staring at them as if they were walking out of her life forever instead of merely wading into the water.

"Oh, for goodness' sake, Fiona," he exclaimed. "Do you think I'm goin' t' let him be swept away from me? If you're that worried about the lad, come in with us an' keep him safe!"

"You know I can't swim, Colin McCoy." She made it an accusation, but at whom he wasn't certain.

"All th' more reason for you t' be in here with us." He gestured. "Get that dress off an' come inta th' water. I'll teach you t' swim an' then we'll both teach th' lad."

"Colin!"

"No one's goin' t' see."

"How can you be so sure?"

Colin sighed. "Tell your mama what I told you, Liam."

"Da asked Mr. Cormac t' put a footman on da paf t' da pond," Liam piped up obediently. "T' make sure no one bovvered us while we're smimmin'."

"Nevertheless, I don't…"

"Aithur come in or be quiet," Colin ordered, shortly.

"I can't get out o' this corset by myself." Reluctantly Fiona got to her feet. "Besides, Liam shouldn't see…"

"My God, th' lad's three. Do you think he's going t' remember this? Besides, he's already seen your risin beauties more times than I have, when he nursed. Come, Liam." Colin stepped back onto the bank.

"Ain't we gonna smim?" Liam asked.

"Not just yet. I'm going t' help your mama out o' her clothes so she can swim while you sit on th' bank an' watch." Colin lifted the child, placing him on a large boulder near the pond's edge.

"But, Da…"

"…an' then I'll teach you an' we'll have a high ol' time splashin' an' chasin' fish." He stalked away to where Fiona waited.

Oblivious of his nakedness, Liam perched obediently on the boulder as Colin unbuttoned Fiona's gown, unlaced her corset, and very slyly wiggled his hand inside her pantalettes and patted her backside before helping her slide everything off.

"Close your eyes, Liam," she called out as her gown fell to the grass.

Obediently, Liam put fat fingers over his eyes. Hands to her breasts, Fiona dashed to the pond's edge and splashed into the water.

"Ooh! It's cold!"

"Good, that ought t' get your circulation goin'." Colin scooped up the garments and dropped them over his own, then said, "You can take your hands from over your eyes, lad, an' sit right there until I say you can come into th' water."

"All wight, Da." Liam settled himself on the stone, drawing up his legs and resting his chin on his knees.

Colin ran down the bank and into the water where Fiona waited.

"You're certain no one will…"

"I swear." He put his arms around her and kissed her. "Don't worry, lass." He glanced back at Liam, who looked like a garden cherub perched upon his rock. "Lord, wish th' lad wasn't here. I'd like t' make love t' you in th' water."

"Colin…"

"But I know when t' be indiscreet an' when not…an' when me son's sittin' a few feet away is definitely th' latter." He waded behind Fiona. "Now then, lass, just place yourself in me capable hands an' I'll have you swimmin' like a mermaid in no time."

It took a bit more than "no time," but within two hours Fiona was able to paddle by herself to the point where Colin called to Liam, "See how well your mama swims? Now 'tis your turn, lad."

Liam was off the rock and galloping toward him before he'd finished speaking. He didn't stop at the bank but launched himself into the air. Colin caught him, stumbling backward into deeper water and whirling the child around. Liam's feet stuck the surface, sending water spraying, wetting Fiona, who was in his path.

She squealed, dodging, then began to laugh.

"That's th' spirit," Colin said approvingly. He looked at Liam, who was clinging to his neck, little body floating. "I think Mama's finally beginnin' t' like it."

Fiona waded toward them. The water at that point was up to her breasts, far below Colin's collarbones.

"Now then," he said. "Let's make this lad inta a water baby."

Afterward, convinced Liam was now proficient enough to save himself should he fall into a water trough or tumble from the little dock into the pond, and also promising Fiona the child would never be allowed to go alone into the water until he was at least twelve, Colin waded from the lake announcing his instruction was a success. He pulled a towel from the picnic hamper, dried and redressed Liam and then himself. Setting the hamper a few feet away, he moved the blanket Fiona had been sitting upon, then gave Liam the task of setting out the picnic lunch.

While the child was doing that, Colin motioned for

Fiona to come out of the water. As quickly as possible, he got her dressed again, even if she was perhaps a bit damper than she'd have liked because of the hasty drying she was given when Liam once glanced their way.

"Thank you, lass." Colin kissed her on the cheek as they settled onto the blanket and Liam passed out sandwiches.

"For what?" Fiona bit daintily into the sandwich she took from her son.

"For remindin' me again how toothsome a bit you are." Colin accepted a sandwich from Liam also. "An' thank *you,* son."

"Colin, please..." Fiona nodded at Liam who appeared engrossed in eating his sandwich.

"Ah, th' lad doesn't know what I meant..." Colin began.

"Da, what's toofsome?" Liam stopped eating to ask. "Did someone bite Mama?"

Colin ignored Fiona's triumphant glance as he thought of a quick answer.

****

Supper that night was a bright affair as Fiona and Màiri chattered on about Liam learning to swim.

"Are you goin' t' tell how *you* learned, also?" Colin whispered, eyes gleaming.

"No, and you'd better not, either," she snapped. "Else I may decide to move into that bedchamber Father Quinton told me is mine."

"You'll hear naithin' out o' me," Colin declared, and decided it was prudent to change the subject. "What news tonight, Da? Are the Americans still fightin' amongst themselves? Or has the North finally won o'er the South?"

"I'm so glad Nebraska is out west and Padraig won't be included in the fray," Màiri said.

"As a matter o' fact," Quinton held up an envelope. "I've received another letter from our ithir son."

Shortly after Padraig's announcement of his wedding, Quinton had begun referring to him that way. Now Padraig was no longer a distant relative but once again Quinton's son, if a still absent one.

"It contains some very important news."

"He hasn't enlisted in one of the armies, has he?" Màiri immediately assumed the worse.

"I doubt that, Mama," Colin put in. "Don't you know Padraig's more a lover than a fighter?"

"Colin, what a thing to say about your brother." Màiri looked shocked.

"If I may, I'll read it and you can learn of Padraig's news," Quinton said.

Quinton Aloysius Francis Xavier McCoy, Esquire
McCoy Hall
Tipperary, Ireland
The United Kingdom of Great Britain
Most Honoured Father,

It is my proud duty to inform you that this branch of the McCoy family has been increased by one. Maria has given birth to a son.

I have taken the liberty of naming him Cuilline Padraig Quinton McCoy, after my mother's maiden name and you, sir. I hope you approve.

As to who the child resembles, I wish I might say he's my image but you'll probably be relieved to learn that is not the case. In truth, he resembles Uncle Seamus, having dark hair and eyes which I believe will be hazel. Since Maria is Spanish but could also be mistaken for

Black Irish, this shouldn't be a surprise.

Be happy for me, sir, and I hope someday I may be welcomed back into your home so you and your grandson may meet.

Your son,
Padraig Aloysius Francis McCoy
The Shamrock Ranch
McCoy's Crossing, Nebraska Territory
United States of America

"So now you've two McCoy grandsons," Colin said, as Quinton set down the letter.

"Aye, but one's an American," Quinton pointed out. "Doubt I'll ever see th' lad unless Padraig sends me a daguerreotype or such."

"Now, Da, you ne'er can tell. Didn't he say he hopes someday you'll meet?"

"Guess we'll have t' wait an' see," Quinton replied. "After all, while that country's in the middle o' a war no one's going t' be doin' any travellin' anywhere. For a while, at least." He looked startlingly worried. "I understand they have ironclad ships they use t' sink th' blockade runners bringin' in supplies. Who knows what would happen if they decided t' turn one o' those on a clipper crossin' th' Atlantic?"

"I suppose they might," Colin agreed. "Donal wrote there have been Southerners arrivin' in London tryin' t' get British support. Who's t' say th' Yankees wouldn't sink an English ship if they thought 'twas carryin' supplies t' th' Rebels?"

"Oh, Colin, please. Don't even think such a thing," Màiri begged.

"Sorry, Mama." Colin fell silent.

Thinking of Padraig's letter, he was damned glad

Liam had been born first, even if earlier than he'd hoped to have a child. At least, his brother hadn't upped him in the fatherhood department. Then he chided himself for being so petty, but…it was a good feeling, nonetheless, even if he didn't say so aloud.

****

That night, as they were snuggling in bed, Colin said, "Fiona, love, I've been thinkin'…" When she didn't answer, he asked, "Aren't you goin' t' make some facetious remark?"

"No," she said. "For I've been thinkin', too."

"About what?"

"About why we haven't had another child."

Colin rolled over to stare at her. "Truly, we two are in harmony in our thoughts, for that was what I've been considerin', too."

"Did you come to any conclusions?"

"Nay, except that 'tis a good thing Padraig has a son since we don't seem about t' produce anaithur anytime soon. Do you suppose 'tis God's way o' punishin' us for makin' certain we didn't have a second babe until we wanted one?" He looked down, studying the edge of the sheet.

"I don't have an answer, Colin but I've feared that same thing. After all, we both committed a sin…very deliberately."

"Why didn't you say somethin' before now?"

"Because I was being selfish. I wanted to give Liam all my attention until he was older and now that I'm ready for another baby…" She shook her head.

"Maybe there's somethin' in th' McCoy seed that's gotten weak," Colin ventured. "Liam looks healthy enough…but…perhaps…perhaps all me vitality went inta makin' him an' there's naithin' left for anaithur child. Perhaps…ah, what do I know o' such thin's? I guess we'll simply have t' keep tryin', an if we're not blessed again, then we'll be grateful we have Liam."

He looked thoughtful.

"I was hopin' t' give our son th' joy o' havin' braithurs, but…" Another thought came to mind. "If only Padraig were here instead o' across an ocean. 'Twould be nice if Liam and his cousin Cuilline could meet. Th' two o' them could be as close as braithurs instead o' cousins."

"Perhaps Padraig will come back."

"I doubt that. Da sent him away and Padraig won't come home unless Da asks him. If Da did that, it'd be admittin' he made a mistake. Quinton McCoy's proud, Fiona. You know that. He'll ne'er do such a thin'."

Putting his arms around her, he hugged her and kissed her temple.

"Goodnight, love." Silently to himself, he thought, *Ah, Padraig, I wish you were here, or I were there. I miss you, braithur, an' I want our lads t' meet. I think we all need each aithur.*

Chapter 29

Spring, 1870

One morning, Colin woke up to a startling reality.

Damn. He stared at his reflection in his shaving mirror. *I'm now se'en-an'-thirty. One moment, I'm a blushin' bridegroom, th' next I've been married for nine years. When did it happen?*

The man in the mirror was still hale and hearty, slender and not gone to seed or putting on weight as some did after hitting their prime. Though Liam was still their only child, he felt no loss at their lack of family. If anything, Colin believed he, Fiona, and their son were closer because of that.

Colin still clerked for Quinton, but now he was more an assistant steward than a mere accountant. Though Quinton was by no means elderly, being as yet not quite sixty, he gladly relinquished more of his responsibilities to his son.

Colin often took his place in riding to the farms to collect the rents, as well as standing in arbitration between the tenants and Lord Alisdaire, who was still very absentee in spite of having a grandson in Tipperary. That was a definite bonus for the farmers, since His Lordship was Colin's father-in-law. That made him more apt to come around to Colin's way of thinking on certain issues.

Colin should've been content and he knew this. He told himself he should've been happy. He had a wife whom he still loved as passionately as on their first night together. He had a son of whom he was proud, even if Liam was proving to be a bit of a scamp because he was so spoiled, though at the same time so well-mannered everyone brushed aside his little misadventures. His parents were both alive and healthy and his work wasn't all that demanding.

Nevertheless, he found himself restless on occasion, discontented and uneasy. Some little worm of dissatisfaction was hatching in his heart.

It hadn't come on immediately but seemed to have built up over the years. Gradually, Colin found himself disliking things he'd always done and had taken for granted. He actually caught himself occasionally wishing for some minor disaster to liven up the day. Though immediately regretful of having such a thought, he admitted his life was so ordinary it was dull.

He told himself everyone felt this way at one time or another. One fell into a routine, doing the same thing day in and day out. Hadn't it been that way when he was in school? Though there had been so much happening then, what with classes and studies and the discovery of subjects, he wasn't as aware of it. There were also drinking bouts at the snugs, and the times when Donal took his younger brother under his wing, with trips to brothels. No, his younger life hadn't been as dreary as that of his adult self's.

I'm tired, Colin realized...*tired of wakin' in th' morning an' comin' down t' breakfast...o' eatin' with th' same people e'ery day...seatin' meself behind that desk an' studyin' figures for hours...then stoppin' for luncheon, tea, an' supper...an' goin' t' bed...God forgive me...I'm even tired o' makin' love t me wife e'ery night!*

This latter shocked him until he realized he wasn't tired of making love to Fiona but simply that the setting was becoming so ordinary.

If only we could go away again, just th' two o' us...do somethin' wild an' a little darin...like...steal away t' th' pond at midnight an' strip bare an' swim, then make love in th' water... He was certain Fiona wouldn't agree to that, though once he thought of it, he truly wished it would happen. She'd tell him they were an old married couple now and shouldn't be committing acts expected only of young lovers.

I think I understand why faithful men stray. The idea of doing that to add a little spice to his life never entered his mind, however.

At present, the only thing giving him even a modicum of variety was being with Liam. Teaching his son to ride and shoot, the late afternoons when they'd return to the pond and swim...those were the bright spots in his life.

Colin liked to think he and his son were friends. He knew the child was lonely. Liam often felt the solitariness of being an only child, he was certain. Bridget's children were so much older—the youngest being thirteen now to Liam's eight—that even when they came to visit, they had little to do with the child. As the grandson of the lord's estates manager, it wouldn't do for him to associate too closely with any children from the farms. Liam had to keep himself entertained by reading, playing with his toys, or riding his pony, but those were solitary pursuits, something one person could do. He rarely had any activity in which he participated with others.

Colin feared his son would grow up a misfit, that when it was time for him to go away to school, he'd be socially awkward. Either that or he'd be so reckless and wild at finding himself in the company of other young men his age, and so eager to be accepted, he'd fling himself with abandon into whatever devilment they planned.

I wish Padraig were here. I wish he lived closer.

That would solve everything. Liam and young Cuilline were close enough in age, only about two and a half years separating them. Colin was certain if the cousins were around each other for long, they'd be the closest of friends. In his mind's eye, he could see the two riding their ponies across the meadows behind McCoy Hall, climbing and sliding down haystacks, and...yes, even stealing pastries Cook set on the windowsill to cool.

Damn it, Padraig, why did you have t' be such an embarrassment? I miss you.

Even after all this time, he thought often of his brother, in spite of his petty jealousies.

They had been closer than he and Donal, though he and his elder brother formed a bit of a bond while Colin was at Eton and now, especially after Donal shared his secret.

I wonder if Padraig might consider sendin' Cuilline t' school here when he's older. To Eton, perhaps, then to Oxford where his father had gone? Could Americans be admitted to one of those stately halls of British academe?

Colin began to hatch a scheme. *Padraig could send his son an' I'd send Liam an' th' two would meet an' become friends...* That would be too late. Liam needed someone his own age *now*.

Though Padraig's letters were few and far between, Colin listened avidly to each as it was read by Quinton at the supper table. Padraig never answered the few letters he'd sent. He merely included replies to Colin in correspondence to his father. Because of that, Colin soon stopped writing personally.

Hearing his brother's words, he felt a sudden envy almost bordering on anger… W*hy did* I *have t' be th'* good *son? Why couldn't I be more a rebel, so Da would send me away, too?*

It was a foolish thought. As he considered it, Colin realized he was too family-oriented. He'd spent his entire life trying to live down Padraig's reputation, to convince everyone he hadn't taken after his profligate brother. He'd been obedient and did what he was told.

Even when he was away at school, he hadn't been a troublemaker. Donal might've been a secret rogue and Padraig the blatant wastrel, but he, Colin McCoy… Even when visiting a brothel or getting foxed at a tavern with his chums, he'd never overdone it. He'd returned home to show his true colors by marrying and settling down to raise a family and work with his father, and now…

He was the *good McCoy lad*. That title had been attached to him. Whenever he was introduced, no matter where or to whom, it was he they referred to by that epithet.

I envy Padraig so…

With a pang, Colin realized he wanted to escape his humdrum, very safe life. He'd never taken a chance at anything, not even marrying Fiona had been much of a risk though he hadn't felt that way at the time. Abruptly, he wanted to run away, travel to that far off treeless country where savages roamed the plains and cows stampeded, where one might find danger and excitement simply by stepping out his front door.

That was why, after supper on a day that had been particularly trying for no reason other than that it was so ordinary and exactly like the one before it, and probably the one following it would be the same, the humdrum tediousness of his life struck Colin like a solid blow to his gut.

Quinton had mentioned that with the war in America now over, a railroad was being built connecting one side of that country with the other. It was going through Nebraska, which had now attained statehood.

Colin reacted with a sudden jerk and a grunt, making his father stare at him.

"Something th' matter, lad?"

"Uh, no, sir." For some reason, the existence of the railroad seemed to bother him most of all.

"Not gettin' a touch of dyspepsia, are you? Cook won't like that."

"Nothing like that, sir.

After that, Colin sat at the supper table, watching the footmen serve the meal, seeing Cormac pour the wine. He picked at his food, though it was good as always, and, somewhere during the fifth course, he decided he'd had enough of his current life.

Padraig's out there, in a new state, seein' men build a railroad crossin' from one side o' th' country t' th' aithur, an' I sit here, listenin' to me faithur talk about it.

He looked around at his parents, at his loving wife, and felt his hands clench into fists. He wanted to stand and shout exactly that, perhaps lift his wine goblet and dash it against the hearth, sending crystal shards and wine spattering and shattering…

…and make everyone stare at you as if you've gone mad? His conscience finished for him.

He couldn't do that. Wouldn't.

Instead, he finished his meal like a gentleman should, waited until his father retired to his study for a bit of brandy and a cigar, then followed him, asking permission to enter. As always. At the age of thirty-seven, still being the *good lad.*

"O' course, son," Quinton lowered his cigar. "What is it?"

"Da…" Colin took a deep breath. Abruptly, he felt as he had on one of those rare occasions when he'd misbehaved and been called before his father to answer for it. "I…"

"Is something th' matter, lad?"

"Yes, sir, there is." Colin decided there was no way but to simply say it. "That, for one thing."

"*That?*" Quinton repeated, looking around. "What?"

"Your callin' me *lad.* I'm near se'en-an'-thirty, sir, an' that in no way, shape, or form makes me a *lad.*"

"I know that," Qinton answered amiably, "but you'll always be a lad t' me. I still call Donal that," he pointed out. "An' he's o'er forty now. Probably would say th' same thing t' Padraig if he were here," he added.

"Padraig…" Thankful Quinton had given him an opening, Colin hurried on, "That's anaithur thing. Da, I want t' see Padraig."

"Afraid that's a bit o' an impossibility," Quinton answered. He picked up his cigar and puffed on it. "Your braithur's in America."

"I know, an' I want t' go see him."

"'Tis a long way t' visit, la…Colin." At Colin's

scowl, Quinton changed what he'd been about to say. "Across an ocean. It'd take months t' actually get there. Would you want t' leave Fiona an' Liam that long?"

"I'd take Liam an' Fiona with me. I think Liam needs t' meet his cousin. He needs t' see someone his own age."

"I know 'tis lonely for th' lad, what with there bein' no ithirs his age around, but then he'd have t' leave Cuilline an' come home. How would that feel? If they become friends?"

"He wouldn't have t' leave Cuilline," Colin said. His heart began to pound. *This is it. I have t' say it.* "If I go t' America, Da, I'd go with th' idea o' not comin' back."

Quinton stared at him. It was several moments before he spoke.

"You'd leave your home…your maithur, an' me…t' live in that savage place?"

"Yes, sir."

"I see." Very carefully, Quinton returned the cigar to the ashtray and sat staring at it. He shook his head. "Are you not happy, son? You've a home here as long as you want it. Do you wish your own place? If so, that can be arranged."

"It's not that, Da. I'm happy livin' here, or at least I was… But…"

"Aye, *but*…'tis th' work then." Quinton struggled to understand. "You ne'er really wanted t' be me clerk, you merely did it for Fiona's sake."

"Nay, Da. 'Tisn't that, not completely." Colin struggled to say what was in his heart. "It's…damn it, Da, 'tis so difficult t' explain."

"I'd appreciate it if you'd try," Quinton said quietly.

"Tell me why me son, me quiet well-behaved boy, suddenly wants t' abandon his home an' his country for some place he's only heard o' in letters? Some place so dangerous?"

"That's it...exactly." Colin spoke so abruptly his words seemed a cry. "Because I'm th' quiet one, th' *good* one. All me life, I've been th' one havin' 't overcome what Padraig did. When I was at school, even if Padraig didn't go t' Cambridge, it seemed e'eryone knew o' his escapades. Donal helped a little, but all th' ithirs, it was as if they were waiting t' see if I'd top him in bein' a scandal. Even now, when someone asks about Padraig, they compare me t' him." His voice dropped, mimicking someone else. "*Ah, now, but Colin's th' good McCoy lad. He stayed here. He didn't cause any trouble.*"

He went to the decanter on the mantel, selecting one and splashing wine into a glass, tilted it and drank hurriedly, coughing as the alcohol seared his throat.

"I know this is goin' t'hurt you, sir..."

"Hurt your maithur more," Quinton answered. "Have you thought what this'll do t' her? An' what about Fiona an' th' lad?"

"Fiona's me wife. She'll go wher'e'er I say. As for Liam... He's so young he'll see it as an adventure. Da, can you understand?" Colin returned to where Quinton sat, holding out his hands as if begging.

"I'm sorry t' admit it but I *do* understand." Quinton shook his head. "Once I had th' same thoughts. Guess I can say so now. I suppose all young men do at one time or anaithur, an' those who do it...I wanted t' go far away. Not t' America, but t' India. Uncle Seamus had been there, you know, an' his stories...I wanted t' see the dark-skinned people wearin' those turbans, an' th' snake charmers an' th' tigers. Me faithur convinced me ithirwise...*Stay here, lad, marry an' settle yourself where 'tis safe...don't go t' live in some country where there's fevers an' poisonous snakes an' rebellions.* I was a bit wild in me youth, so I reasoned perhaps 'twas time I settled down. So, I did as he asked." He looked at his son and smiled. "An' regretted it every day o' me life, though it did earn me a wife I love an' children I adore."

He got to his feet.

"Don't go, lad. 'Tis as you say. You're me good boy, an' I don't want t' lose you, too. I don't want you t' take me grandson away. He's me heir, Colin. I need him here."

"We can talk about that when th' time comes," Colin especially didn't want to be swayed by the idea of Quinton dying and possession of the estates in limbo. "Liam loves you, Da. He'll probably want t' come back when he's older."

It might be a lie, but Colin tried to make it a salve to Quinton's loss.

"Aye, th' lad's got a mind o' his own." Briefly, Quinton perked. "He just might. He took a deep breath. "I'd rather naithur o' you went."

He stopped as if thinking a moment and walked to the mantel where he copied Colin's earlier action, pouring brandy from a decanter. Quinton sipped slowly, replacing his glass upon the mantel.

"What if I forbid you t' go?" He whirled to look back at his son, voice rising threateningly. "What if I say straight-out, *Colin, take me grandson away an' I'll disinherit you?*" He looked as if he'd played a winning card in a game with very high stakes, certain he'd won.

"You won't do that," Colin sounded just as sure.

"Nay? Try me and see. Think you could support a wife an' child on naithin'?"

"That'll simply be more reason for me t' go t' America," Colin answered. "I understand exiles an' th' disenfranchised are welcome there."

"Damn it, son." Anger made an edge to Quinton's words as his bluff was called. "You can't do this."

"I'm sorry, Da, but I can, an' I will." Colin's answer was firm.

"Don't make me beg." Quinton's next words were startlingly quiet.

"Me mind's made up." Colin spoke softly as if to raise his voice might shatter something delicate. "I'm not askin' your permission t' go, but I would like t' leave with your blessin'." He smiled. "Who knows? I may not like th' place an' you'll find me back here with me tail 'twixt me legs, clerkin' away at me desk as usual."

"I doubt that." Quinton snorted. "You've got th' McCoy stubbornness for all your obedience, an' I don't think you'd admit it even if you hated what you find."

He caught Colin in a surprising embrace, hugging his son to his chest.

"So now I've got t' find anaithur clerk? I'm too old t' be doin' these accounts meself."

"Ask Phelan," Colin suggested. "He and I were at th' top o' our classes. Now that he's married an' settled, he might be glad t' help out."

Quinton released him, blinking slightly, green eyes damp. Colin knew he'd never let the first tear fall, however.

"When would you want t' leave?" He was all business now, but resignation was in the question.

"I don't know th' ship schedules." With departure

an accomplished fact, Colin had a momentary twinge of regret. He forced himself to ignore it. "I'll have t' check."

Quinton nodded. "Know that if you wish t' come back, we'll be here waitin' for you."

"Thank you, Da." Colin turned.

"Son…"

He looked back.

"I'll miss you."

Colin didn't dare speak. Nodding, he ran from the study.

He didn't see Quinton go to the mantel and take down the decanter and refill his glass to the rim.

"Oh, God…what did I do…t' deserve havin' all me sons go so far away?"

****

Fiona was in their bedroom. She wasn't ready for bed but was sitting by the hearth, embroidering the McCoy monogram on a pillowslip. Colin stood in the doorway watching her pale fingers as they pushed the needle in and out, making tiny stitches blend together in a delicate pattern swirling around to form the upstroke of the M.

She looked up and saw him. "Colin, how long have you been standing there?"

"Long enough." He hurried over, taking the embroidery hoop from her hands and dropping it onto the divan as he sat beside her. "Fiona, I've been thinkin'."

"About what?"

"You know, 'tis been quite some time since we've been alone."

"What does that mean?" She gave him an askance look. "We're alone every night. Here in our bedroom.

And from the way you act, I'm glad of it." She laughed. "I'd truly hate for either your mother or father to know how passionate you are, my dear husband."

"You still love me then? After all this time?"

"What kind of question is that? Of course I still love you. We've been sleeping in the same bed for nine years, haven't we?

"Thank you for that, love." He relaxed, slightly. "Because it makes what I'm going t' say a bit easier."

"What's that?" Briefly, she looked worried. "You're not going to tell me you've tired of my company, are you?"

He didn't answer.

"Colin?"

"Nay, lass, I'll ne'er tire o' you, but there's ithir thin's… Fiona, I made a decision t'night."

"Oh?"

"I'm goin' abroad. *We're* goin', I should say."

"A trip? Oh, Colin, how wonderful." She smiled, leaning toward him. "And here you had me so worried. I didn't want to say anything, but I'd really like to get away for a while. We haven't traveled together since our wedding trip to Paris. Where are we going? Back to Paris?"

"No."

"To Rome…or Florence? Naples, perhaps?" She was naming all the places she'd heard others speak of. "Wait…*see Naples and die*…I wouldn't want to do that last part."

"Fiona…we're not goin' t' France or Italy."

"Where then? How long will we be gone? Two weeks, three? Oh!" She frowned, worried. "We can't leave Liam for that long. Though I suppose Mother Màiri and the nanny can care for him. After all, it isn't as if he's an infant. I certainly wouldn't leave him if he were."

"We'll take Liam with us."

"Of course, why didn't I think of that? Even though it won't be as romantic with a child in tow. In fact, with the nanny, and Geoffrey and Edith, we're not going to be alone at all." She looked rueful. "Just as it was on our wedding trip." There was a sigh. "I suppose it can't be helped, however."

"Fiona…"

"Truly, Colin, I wish we could simply slip away by ourselves, board a packet and sail around for a month or two with no destination in sight."

"Fiona, dearest…"

"I suppose that's a foolish idea. One always has to have an arrival point, doesn't one?" She looked toward the wardrobe. "I wonder if I need to buy new traveling clothes?"

"Fiona." Colin caught her hands, squeezing them tightly. "Listen t' me."

"Colin, what is it? You look…" She pulled a hand free, touching his cheek. "I don't know…distracted?"

"Fiona, we're goin' t' America."

"America? But who do we know in…oh." She bit her lip, looked away, then smiled slightly. "Padraig? We're going to visit Padraig?"

Not visit, but t' stay…if I like th' place. He didn't say that aloud, better to leave that for later, when he'd seen how things were in Nebraska. Still, if what Fiona was saying was true, and she wanted to get away as sincerely as he did…

He nodded.

"It'll take quite some time to get to Nebraska, I

imagine. Months crossing the ocean and then going west."

"Aye."

"I've never actually been on an ocean voyage. I hope I don't get *mal-de-mer*."

"You didn't when we crossed th' Channel," he reminded her.

"The Channel isn't a *real* ocean," she retorted. "I didn't consider that a *voyage*. What about your work with the estates? Is Father Quinton all right with this? Can he be without you that long?"

"He'll have t' be," he answered. "I'm a grown man, not a child he can order around."

Her expression said he was a long time in deciding that, but she didn't say it aloud.

"I told him I wished t' see me braithur. I want Liam t' meet his cousin. It'll be good for him. It'll be good for us, too, t' get away from here, to be alone, on our own."

"I'd like to say I'm not surprised, but I am. I knew you missed your brother. I would've had to be blind not to see the wistful look on your face whenever Father Quinton reads one of his letters aloud, but…Colin, I never once thought of suggesting such a thing."

"But you *are* willing t' go? You want t' go with me?"

"Willing? What a way to put it. Of course, I want to go with you. Goodness, you make it sound as if we're running away or something." She pulled him toward her, kissing him gently. "It's a little late to be eloping, dear."

Is it? Colin wondered. *Perhaps I* am *runnin' away. Good God. At th' age of thirty-se'en, I'm runnin' away from home!*

He felt such an excitement stirring within him for a

moment, he felt as if he'd cry out with the sheer joy of it, as well as the dread—of seeing something new, something unknown. There was an anticipation he hadn't experienced since that night in the hunting lodge, as he faced a different unknown, when he became a husband.

Aye, a husband but not th' head o' me own house.

In America, he'd be that and more, and he'd have his wife and his son, and his brother to share a new life.

The good McCoy lad was at last kicking over the traces. Colin was about to do something outrageous. He was going to begin his long-awaited adventure.

Author's Notes

Arsenic dresses: An informative description of the use of arsenic to create a specific green color used to dye fabric, and the health issues it caused, can be found at: https://jezebel.com/the-arsenic-dress-how-poisonous-green-pigments-terrori-1738374597

A word about the author…

Toni V. Sweeney has lived thirty years in the South, a score in the Middle West, and a decade on the Pacific Coast, and now she's trying for her second thirty on the Great Plains.

Since the publication of her first novel in 1989, Toni has written 94 novels, with 89 of them being published. This includes several series.

https://www.facebook.com/profile.php?
id=100048587829251

Thank you for purchasing
this publication of The Wild Rose Press, Inc.

For questions or more information
contact us at
info@thewildrosepress.com.

The Wild Rose Press, Inc.